Previous Books in
The Unspoken Series
by Marilyn Grey

Book #1

Where Love Finds You
Ella & Matthew

Book #2

Down from the Clouds
Gavin

Book #3

The Life I Now Live
Heidi & Patrick

HEART ON A
Shoestring

MARILYN GREY

WINSLET
PRESS

WINSLET PRESS

Heart on a Shoestring
Copyright © 2014 by Marilyn Grey

To learn more about Marilyn Grey, visit her Web site:
www.marilyn-grey.com

Library of Congress Control Number:

ISBN-10: 0985723548
ISBN-13: 978-0985723545

Cover & Interior Design by Tekeme Studios

Printed in the United States of America

First Edition: January 2014
14   12   11   10   9   8   7   6   5   4   3   2   1

To:
Kristyn Magness

For:
quite simply: being weird

extended version:

Who could've possibly imagined we'd still be friends after our AOL friendship blossomed in a sweaty gym class. We also can't forget the prologue. Peach Oatmeal. Your desk. First grade. Some things are meant to be cherished. So, why am I dedicating this book to you, of all books? Well, because I'm weird like Miranda and you have a deep appreciation for strange people. It's not just that though. You accept the least of us with open arms. You can handle a passionate fiery person who constantly tells you to stop eating the poison and still be her friend. You can handle angry rat faces and sarcasm with delight. You are a passionate person yourself, a dreamer, a wife, a mother, a friend, a daughter, and a huge encouragement to people like me. Since day one, you've read my silly attempts at writing a novel. You cheered me on from the start. You are the first person to read every book I've written. Every time. You are an amazing person in so many ways and I can't thank you enough on this short little page. You are a lovely person and an even lovelier friend. I hope we have many more years together. One day, when we're old, if we make it, I'd like to have conversations about J. Holmes and organic milk, simply because you're the one person who would. Thank you for being weird too. Weird people appreciate weird people like you wouldn't believe. Across the miles, I scream out to you loud enough to scare the birds in the tree outside of my window:

THANK YOU

*Dreaming of the person you want to be is
wasting the person you already are.*
Kurt Cobain

*Not until we are lost do we
begin to understand ourselves.*
Henry David Thoreau

*Everybody's at war with different things.
I'm at war with my own heart sometimes.*
Tupac Shakur

Chapter One
Miranda

Some people spend their lives walking by people on benches, while others spend their lives sitting on benches analyzing the people walking by. My friends would say I'm the one racing by the lonely bench sitters, candy pink hair tossed in the wind, dreams clutched in my shoulder bag, stars in my eyes, but I'm not.

I know, it's shocking.

Once again, streetlights twinkled in the early summer air as I sat on another iron park bench. The best place on earth. At least to me. The place where people became stories and stories became dreams and dreams sparked the hidden echoes of my heart. All on a paint-chipped park bench.

An older woman jogged by and stepped on someone's lost newspaper, crumpling it and sending it flopping down the path behind her. One persons hard work, another's doormat. I turned my head and watched her jog into the clouds, back to her smiling newborn and eager husband, back to the beauty of her family.

She passed a young couple huddled together, shivering in the nighttime chill. They walked by me, laughing, her head tilted back against his chest, eyes on the budding tree branches above them, their love story unfolding like a handwritten note from a seventh grade crush. Excitement abounds. His arm, tight around her waist, and the frown on his face when she checked her phone, showed his possessiveness. But the cherry lipstick mark an inch from the corner of his mouth showed that she liked being owned as much as he liked owning her.

I listened. Watched. Breathed in and adored all that lived around me. Around me. Always around me. I so envied the world around me. Don't get me wrong, I loved my own life too, but that didn't stop me from wishing I could close my eyes and slip into someone else's life. You know, explore the world with different eyes, a different heart.

Another couple walked by, swinging hands in the breeze. A ring sparkled on her left hand, but not his. Engaged. Judging by their excitement, he proposed recently. He looked ahead as they passed me. Her eyes met mine, then she turned to make sure he wasn't looking at me too. Funny. Her insecurity would sure enough wilt their relationship. Odd considering her preoccupation with herself seemed more important than him. Her awkward five inch heels and layers of makeup made it obvious. When he tried to touch her hair she pulled back and rearranged it. Perhaps she had mistaken the eyes of lust for the beat of his heart. They walked into a growing fire. Soon their swinging hands would fall to their sides as she consumed herself with dresses and flowers and cakes. Everything but her beloved. The beginning of the end. The end of their bliss. The beginning of struggles and conflicts and maybe, just maybe, their love would triumph through it all.

Rare though.

I'm not cynical, I swear. You can call the sky blue or you can find a way to make yourself believe it's green, but in the end it's still blue. I'm not afraid to see blue even when it's not the most appealing. Love is hard. It's not easy to make love to a person only to find out that their very person is chipping away the rotted parts of your person, making you into something better, but often in the most excruciating ways. That's when most people run. But hey, that's love. Becoming one. Being one. Living as one and morphing your soul into the soul of another.

Then, there's marriages like my parents have....

A group of high school kids walked by. Joking and stepping on each others shoe laces while slapping gum and spraying out a colorful array of cuss words like graffiti on the walls of life. Heads held high, shoulders back. Maybe juniors. Just on the brink of saying goodbye to their senior friends and claiming the role themselves. The ever coveted senior status. When you think you're the coolest thing to walk the locker-lined halls, when really you're just like everyone else. A puppet in the game of life. Controlled by everything around you and not enough inside you.

I stood and walked away from the bench, becoming a passer by. I nodded to each empty bench I passed, bowed, said hello, and kept walking.

Not hello to imaginary friends. Sorry, I'm not that weird. Saying hello to the dreamer that would sit there next, wishing and hoping to slip into the life of a passerby for a minute. Only a minute. To see if the grass is really greener on the other side.

I walked fast, tilted my head back, and stretched out my arms. Couldn't hide my smile if I wanted to. The cool air clung to my cheeks as the stars twinkled above. Enormous fire balls that never moved. Ah, what it would be like to be a huge ball of plasma. So neutral. Yet so exhilaratingly beautiful, held together by your own gravity. Yes, gravity. Stability. Words I had yet to acquaint myself with. I coalesced with no one. Not even myself.

I looked ahead. Dreaming of the day I'd share these thoughts with another soul. It would take a lot for someone to know me. The real me. Not even sure if I did.

Love. It would be hard. Very hard. Breaking down my walls and letting someone in? I don't know. I liked my life. Singleness didn't scare me as much as marriage did. Commitment. Falling in love a thousand times appealed to me more than falling in love once and working to feel in love with that same person every morning and night of my life. For. Ever.

Besides, most guys were far, far too normal for me. And I just can't do normal.

"Oh, are you a southern belle tonight?" a man said.

I turned. Ah, Earl. The skinny homeless man with one half of his dirty button-down shirt tucked in, just like his life. He dreamed to help the world, to do something nobel prize worthy. He always spoke of Rosa Parks and Maya Angelou. But his breath always smelled of Jack Daniels and he could barely help himself off the curb. I scooted my dress out of the way, did a curtsy, and said with my finest southern drawl, "Fancy seeing you here tonight, Mr. Earl. Need some help off thissy here curb?"

He nodded and took my hand. I helped him to the park bench where he leaned back and almost passed out.

"Yesterday you were Irish with blue hair and now you're a southern lady with a huge dress and pink hair," he said. "Unless you are a dream."

"Why, yes, sir. My name is Annabelle and we're back quite a few decades in the state of Georgia." I spun in a circle. "Would you like to see my five step waltz?"

13

"Your five step what?" He mumbled and smiled. "You about the strangest girl I know."

"My pleasure." I bowed and danced away, down the streets of life, right to my apartment door.

Derek called me, but I ignored and skipped up the steps and unlocked my door. He wanted to visit again. He was nice and all. Extremely attractive, in a rugged Johnny Depp kind of way. But strange. And boring. Nothing like his sister, Ella, who saw life through the eyes of Cupid. And I dreamed of a man who would dress up with me and dance the streets of Philadelphia. He barely changed his shirt, much less his mind. I couldn't even convince him to ride a go-kart.

Not my flavor starburst, that's for sure. I wanted a cherry. A little sweet, a little sour, and yum-diddly-licious. He was a lemon. Yellow, but not like the sun. More like a bitter, rotten lemon rind. Did I mention that he was nice though? He was nice. And had a great smile. A great smile he rarely showed.

He texted. I ignored and rolled onto my bed. Feet in the air, hoop dress a flying, I smiled.

Life didn't need a man to be enjoyed. In fact, for me, a man could ruin everything. Take my fun and leave me lifeless.

Mmm, yeah, not ready for such things. Not ready at all.

Chapter Two
Derek

No one, and I mean no one, pissed me off like Miranda did. She flirted like someone playing darts with no hand-eye coordination. Not a lick of aim in her body. A casual flirt who probably gave hundreds of guys the wrong impression, like she obviously did to me, but something drew me to her. No idea why. I swore off women long ago. Marriage? Not for me. That didn't change, but I couldn't help myself. I wanted to see her again. Her odd and dimpled smile and whacked out hair styles. If anything, just to laugh.

I needed to laugh. Work zapped the life out of me like a squirrel eating an electric wire. My parents convinced my sister and I into college. Ella lasted a week. I lasted eight years. Yes. Eight. Don't ask.

Eight years of school and all I had to show for it was a dingy apartment and faded jeans.

Derek Rhodes. Marketing Manager for Doodle Dandy Dog Candy. At your service. Pleased to meet you. How do you like my fake smile? Good. Great. Wonderful.

The only person I can blame is myself. No one, not even my parents, knew my successes or failures. I told no one who I was and what I really did. Even created a fake name and legally changed it. My family knew me as Derek Rhodes. My old colleagues knew me as David Bennett. I kept the two world's separate because I feared the exact thing that happened. Failure. And man, that kind of failure is more than embarrassing. It's flat-out crippling. No one could know David Bennett. I didn't even want to know him. Hated everything he did and loathed his existence.

Yeah. Needed a smile.

Something to take my mind off of what could have been and help me start over. But the girl wouldn't answer her phone. Only when she was bored. According to her I was too normal and only wanted as a last resort. Not like I wanted to get into her pants, just wanted a friend.

Thirty-three years old and spending my life at Doodle Dandy Dog Candy didn't exactly provide the most friendships. And the friends I did have were all married and sprinkled across America. Kids. White picket fences. Minivans.

Miranda could say I was normal all she wanted, but I didn't have kids, a white picket fence, and certainly no minivan. Couldn't fathom driving one of those ghastly things.

A text popped up on my phone screen. Miranda finally responded. *What's going on tonight Mr. Rhodes? Counting the tiles in your ceiling again?*

You are so annoying, I typed back, then erased, and typed, *If you think I'm so boring how about answering your phone so I can live a little?*

Miranda: *Impossible. I've tried. You are not receptive to my ingenious plans.*

Derek: *I'm coming up this weekend and I will be at your house Saturday at noon. If you want to hang out... be there.*

Miranda: *Is the glass half full or half empty?*

Derek: *The glass is a figment of your imagination. See ya Saturday.*

I couldn't figure out if she was genuinely an annoying person or if the age difference made her seem immature. Especially the hair. I can understand dying your hair every so often, but almost every week? And I'm not talking brown or blonde. I'm talking rainbow bright.

Immature, annoying, either way she made me laugh and shake my head. And I needed a break this weekend anyway.

AFTER AN EXHAUSTING DRIVE TO PHILLY, I STOOD IN FRONT of her apartment door, caught my breath, and knocked. A few seconds passed, the door knob wiggled, and the door jerked open to reveal a grinning Princess Leia. A grinning Princess Leia with pink hair.

"What the hell?" I said. "I thought we were going out to eat?"

"What? You don't like?" she said in a hushed Princess Leia tone. "Let's walk the town and pretend we're fighting evil."

"Seriously, Miranda." I shook my head. "Change your clothes."

16

"I'm not changing. You need to change." She pulled the edge of my sleeve. "Brown, brown, brown. Every time I see you. Do you own anything else?" She tugged my hair. "And do you ever wash your hair? I'm all about the Kurt Cobain look if you can make it appealing, but this ain't appealing buddy."

I turned and walked away. Fast and agitated. She yelled from the doorway. "Don't be so boring."

I got in my car, slammed the door, and stared off. Why did I let her frustrate me so much? Her opinions didn't matter. Boring is relative. To an introvert a party with a big group of people is boring. To an extrovert a calm afternoon at the bookstore is boring. I'm not freaking boring, I convinced myself. She didn't even know me. How could she judge who I am based off my shirt choices and lack of desire for roller coasters?

"I'll show her how ridiculous this is," I said to myself, then started the car and made my way to the mall. Took a while to find everything I needed. Once I did, I changed and drove back to her apartment, and threw rocks at her window until she appeared in the doorway, still Princess Leia. I hid from her view, then flapped into sight, light saber glowing in the evening air as I twisted it and turned around as though fighting some invisible person. "Come down, Leia. I am the force. And I am with you."

She covered her mouth with her hands and laughed, then jumped up and down like someone who won the lottery. I waved her down. She held up her hand, ran inside, and returned with her purse and keys.

"Miracle of all miracles," she said, smiling way too much. "No guy has ever dressed up like Han Solo for me."

"No guy ever will again. Seriously, you realize how dumb this is, right?"

"It's fun. And I think you look kinda good like that."

I laughed. "You do this for some kind of validation. It's not normal. If you were truly confident in who you were you wouldn't need to change all the time."

She rolled her eyes and walked back to the steps. I grabbed her arm and forced her to look at me. "See," I said. "You run from what I'm saying because it's true. You don't want to face the person you are so you avoid her by being all these other people."

She jerked her arm from me and stomped up the stairs, making it a point to slam the door as loud as possible. And me. Alone. At the bottom of the steps, wishing I didn't have to be so opinionated. Or at least didn't speak my opinions so much. David Bennett spoke his opinions and every-one loved him. But everyone hated Derek Rhodes whenever he spoke up.

Still. I was right.

Chapter Three
Miranda

I didn't need him and his games. Not even sure who he thought he was. Some kind of god of my life, coming to rescue me from the ditches he envisioned me stuck in.

Thanks, but no thanks.

I changed my clothes and took a shower. My favorite place to calm down. After an hour of processing his words and choosing to ignore them, I grabbed a basket of clothes and took them to the washer near my kitchen. Ah, never put the last round in the dryer. Opened the dryer and something thundered toward me, hissing like a creature of the night.

I fell backwards into the wall, slid to the ground, and narrowed my eyes as my heart shot out of my chest and Derek climbed out of the dryer. I held my hands out and shook my head. Shocked.

"You didn't lock the door." He brushed off his Han Solo outfit. "Surprised I could fit in there. Took you long enough."

"How did you know I'd do laundry?"

"I didn't."

"Then why did you hide in there?"

"Saw your clothes in your room and figured you might catch up. Then I saw the wet clothes in the washer and knew you'd eventually toss them in here."

"You are cruel."

"I can be weird too, you know. I wasn't always the person I am now."

"Apparently."

Cruel prank. Scared the crap out of me. Almost literally too. But I must admit, he instantly earned six double chocolate brownie points for being the opposite of normal. And I actually let him stay a while.

I made two big bowls of ice cream with a thousand and one toppings, then sat beside him on the couch.

He looked at the ice cream and raised his eyebrows.

I shrugged and smiled.

"Where's the ice cream in here?" he said.

"It's mysterious."

He nodded and took a heaping bite of awesomeness as I watched, imagining his pure delight as it surprised his taste buds.

"This is terrible," he said.

I shrunk into the couch and took his bowl. More for me then.

He snatched it back. "For someone so strange you really can't take a joke."

"Guess I don't expect joking from Mr. Ho-Hum."

"You think I believe your facade?"

I stood and walked to the kitchen. He followed.

"I'm serious." He leaned against the counter and pulled a strand of my hair. "You don't even know who you are."

"You don't understand me."

"Does anyone?"

I crossed my arms and squinted, hoping he'd disappear if I crushed him with my eyelids. Like a tiny nat caught in my eye.

"You don't even understand yourself," he said.

"I understand plenty. You just can't fathom someone enjoying life and being positive about everything because for whatever reason you hate the world and most things in it."

"I don't hate the world."

"You never say anything positive. Everyone is always falling apart. Love doesn't last. Dreams fail. The world sucks. You know everything and everyone else knows nothing, unless they agree with you. You complain constantly and you have no desire to change things. You expect me to seek advice from someone like you?"

He slammed his bowl into the sink, his eyes glowing like a hyena on drugs, then walked to my front door and left.

Part of me felt sorry for saying all that, but he had no problem dishing out his opinions, whether they hurt or not. He needed to hear the truth too.

The door opened. He walked up to me, eyes on the ground, mumbling to himself. Still in his hilarious costume. Less than a foot away from me, he stopped, grabbed my face, and looked right into my eyes. My legs weakened. I stepped back and steadied myself on the counter. His eyes searched mine. Looking for some treasure underneath. Not sure what he intended to find. Don't know why, but I didn't realize how much I wanted to kiss him until now. And wow, did I want to kiss his face off until we lit up the room with a million fireworks.

He dropped his hands to his sides and walked out again. I waited for him to come back, my lips urging me to chase him out the door until they landed on him. But I didn't listen. I stood there for a few minutes, picked up my purse, and headed to the place I loved most.

It was cool and crisp. Orion winked at me as I took my usual seat and pulled my legs up to my chest. City air filled with busy sounds could suffocate those accustomed to clean countryside air and only the sound of happy crickets, but it rejuvenated me. Inspired me. Tree branches lit by streetlights and benches marked with old gum and cigarette butts. Something about it. Maybe the stamp of struggle and the fight for triumph. Maybe the man across from me, sucking the life out of his paper-wrapped nicotine, enjoying himself until another man stopped and begged him to trade fifty cents for the rest of his cigarette. He waved the pest away with disgust. I smiled.

Derek sucked the life out of me like that man charred the life out of his lungs. Until him, I questioned nothing and lived most days with a perpetual smile. A perpetual longing for the beauty of life around me. Talking to him was like walking into a wrestling match. I defended myself by ducking or lost it and punched him where it counts. Who wants to have conversations like that?

A father walked by with his daughter saddled high on his shoulders. She pulled his hair to direct the horse as he made sounds and laughed his way to their stable, their stability, their life. I dreamed of such things. My dad, if you could call him that, barely talked to the woman he married, much less his kids. Stability seemed foreign, out of reach for a person like me.

A young girl walked by, dragging her feet and kicking rocks. Could've been me ten years ago. I imagined her walking off into The Big Dipper as her story sparkled and transformed into something wonderful. Something filled with love and laughter as the tree branches waved with delight. To-morrow everyone at school would forget who was popular and who wasn't and love everyone for who they really were. Then she'd get her chance. Then she'd turn her slow walk into an excited skip. Sometimes all we need is a little reason to wake up the next day. That's all it takes to spark the light inside. Just one little reason.

I nodded to the man across from me. He half-smiled, then stood and walked away. I liked it here on these benches. No matter which part of the city I found myself in, I found some kind of story to dream up.

Pencil in hand, tablet on my lap, I started writing the story I longed to live. Page one, first sentence: *When dreams evaporate into the clouds and come back down as tiny rain droplets, are they the same dreams, or something altogether new?*

Chapter Four
Derek

It takes a lot for me to admit when someone else is right. Especially when it cuts open old wounds of mine. But Miranda was right and I couldn't bring myself to tell her. Fear of what people would think—of what I'd think—if I revealed David Bennett to the world, consumed me. The very things I berated Miranda for doing, I did myself. That's why I knew her better than she knew herself.

She was right. And maybe I did need to tell her. If anything, just for the sake of telling another soul and feeling like someone, somewhere, really knew me.

So, I devised a plan. First, I called my boss.

"Hey," I said. "I'm going to need off for two weeks. An emergency came up."

"Two weeks? Sorry, bro. You take off that kind of time and you can kiss this job goodbye."

"Well, consider me puckered up." I made a kissing sound and hung up the phone. So unlike me. More like David Bennett. The thought worried me. I didn't want to be him anymore. I wanted to be the person I was before him or nothing at all.

Okay, so I just randomly quit my job. This must be what she says about living. Truly living. Or was I truly being a stupid person? I couldn't help but wonder.

With plenty of time on my hands, I packed, and planned, and enjoyed the anticipation.

What three things would you want if you were stranded on an island? I texted Miranda.

She responded five minutes later. *An old victorian nightgown. My journal.*

And a pen with blue ink and a fine tip. Why?

No reason, I said. Then grabbed my keys and went out to the nearest antique store, found an old white nightgown with a tag that claimed it was from 1890, bought it for a hundred dollars, then stopped at Walgreens to get a notebook and a pack of pens.

I spent the rest of my night preparing the boat, gathering food and supplies, and barely sleeping. Hopefully she wouldn't mind being kidnapped. She's weird enough, I thought, but you never know.

THE MORNING LIGHT WOKE ME UP, BUT I COULD BARELY OPEN my eyes. A long drive twice in a day, then all that labor with my boat and shopping, man, wiped me out. I forced my eyes open as I stumbled to the shower and got myself ready. I skimmed my closet for something nice to wear. All brown except one plaid button-down shirt. I slipped it on over one of my typical brown shirts, pulled on my nicer jeans, complete with belt, and looked in the mirror. Hmmm, I thought. Maybe time for a haircut.

I shaved off my beard and filled the sink with way more hair than I thought I had on my face. Traded my rugged look for a long-haired Jon Bon Jovi. Not for too long though. I stuffed everything I needed into a backpack and drove to the closest hair salon, told the lady to give me a Keith Urban look, then walked out like a new person hoping to high hell no one noticed me.

When I parked in front of Matt's house a few hours later I inhaled and exhaled and forced myself out of the car. One step, two step, three steps closer to showing her one piece of who I really am. Scared the heck out of me.

I almost went back to the car, but Matt opened the door and narrowed his eyes, looked me up and down, and said, "Gavin, come quick. I think I'm dreaming."

Gavin stood in the doorway and smiled. "Normal looks good on you."

I shook my head and walked passed them, straight to Ella. Weird seeing my little sister pregnant. She lifted her hand from her stomach to hug me, then tousled my hair. "Who ya trying to impress?"

"Just time for a change."

She smirked as though she didn't believe me. I never won any awards for lying or acting. Just for hiding.

Lydia walked over with a newborn wrapped in some kind of fabric contraption on her chest.

"Is that from Africa or something?" I said.

She laughed. "No. It's a Boba Wrap. Never seen one before?"

Seeing a newborn wrenched my heart. Every time. Never failed. I often wondered if I'd ever be able to look at a baby without feeling horrible inside. Worse than horrible actually. The past haunted me in every newborn I saw. Every time. I tried to ignore the little hand all curled up and poking out of that fabric thing, but I couldn't.

The past is the past. But really, is it ever? I spent years ignoring David Bennett. Years ignoring everything tied to him, including Ashleigh. The girl that ruined my life. Well, that's not really fair. I ruined my own life by chasing her. And now I tried to ruin her life by ignoring her, by withholding the resolution she wanted. The ending I wasn't sure I could give. But could I avoid her forever? The past is the past, yes, but it's also part of who I am. Whether I liked it or not. My past was more of me than the future I wished it could be.

"Deep in thought?" Ella said.

I shrugged. Miranda walked in. Hair the color of a lime. Clothes like something out of Flashdance. I liked her. A lot. Fun girl. Amazingly brilliant. But why did she feel the need to hide her stunning beauty behind odd hairstyles and weird clothes? It didn't make sense.

She ignored me until I walked over to her, took her hand, and apologized. A softness replaced her clenched jaw and she squeezed my hand.

"I want to take you somewhere," I said. "Get away for a little. I planned an amazing vacation. You think Dee will be okay without you for a few days?"

"She will. But will we be okay with each other for a few days?"

I nodded, pleading with my eyes, hoping she would come away with me.

Chapter Five
Miranda

Okay, breathe Miranda. This is the same guy that looked like a freak yesterday, I told myself. A freak in a normal way. Now, he looked like something straight out of a Calvin Klein ad. I stopped myself from imagining it. Okay, so I didn't stop myself. Wow. Okay. Breathe.

He asked again. "Will you come or not?"

"When?"

"Right after this party."

"No."

"Tomorrow?"

I shrugged. "Let me think about it."

So, I'm not a judge a book by the cover person. Normally. My favorite books are obscure, have the least intriguing covers, and captivate me because of the story, not the models on the cover. But if I were judging a book by its cover ... The Derek Rhodes Story just moved up to the best sellers list in my world.

I do realize how superficial that sounds. And I'm not normally so shallow, but the guy was beyond gorgeous with all that hair gone. It shocked me. I tried not to watch him across the room as I talked to Ella and Lydia.

"You and my brother are still trying to tell yourselves that you don't like each other?" Ella said. "You haven't stopped staring at him since you got here."

"What happened in his past that made him so strange?"

"Not sure. He went off to college and stopped talking to us for years. He could've been dead for all we know. He came back one day and looked like a different person. Long hair. Beard. Major chip on his shoulder."

"What did he go to school for?"

"Marketing or business or something."

I turned to Lydia as she bounced her baby in the wrap. "What did you name him? I can't remember."

She smiled at the baby and held his hand. "His name is Liam."

I glanced at Derek. He glanced at me. Butterflies.

"What was Derek like in high school?" I said to Ella.

"Intelligent, but stupid."

I laughed. "How so?"

"Let's just say this. He was Prom King and voted Most Likely to Succeed, but behind the scenes he was a major pot head." She turned to him. "He was popular, but maintained his grades and graduated top of the class. All while being known as 'High Roller' because he always found the best marijuana."

I stared at her, possibly blinked a few times.

"I know it's hard to imagine. When he went to college something happened to him. He hasn't been the same since. Won't tell anyone."

"Wow," Lydia said. "Where did he go to college?"

"Don't know. He never told anyone. Strange, but we weren't close at that point so I never asked much. We are closer now, but he won't tell me what happened. Believe me, I've asked a thousand times." She looked at him again. "I always hoped he'd find a girl to show him a different side of life. Help him live a little." She turned to me. "He needs to laugh again."

"No, no," I said. "I'm not the girl."

She grinned and shrugged. I shook my head as she laughed my unwillingness away. As much as I denied her prodding, I admit he intrigued me. A mysterious man who needed to learn to live. Yes. Exactly the kind of thing I liked.

A challenge.

I walked over to him. Engrossed in a conversation about concrete and gravel with the guys, he didn't notice me. I linked my arm with his and smiled. He looked down at me, unlinked his arm, and said, "So you'll go?"

I nodded. "On one condition."

He stepped aside and led me to the kitchen. "What?"

"Once we get there you have to answer every question I have without hiding the truth."

He walked around the kitchen in two circles, then stopped, put his hands in his pockets, and said, "Sorry. I can't do that."

"Then I'm not going."

He shoved his hands deeper into his pockets. "I will tell you some things, but not all."

"Why do you want to go on vacation with me of all people?"

Matt walked in. "Look at you two love buttons."

"More like one ferromagnetic magnet repelling another paramagnet who seems to only have a North Pole and can't seem to align himself with the South Pole of the ferromagnetic magnet." I took a breath. "Actually, no, maybe it's just a case of diamagnetism."

Matt stopped whatever he was doing, hand mid-air, eyes peeled back, and waited for Derek's response.

"It's not diamagneticism." Derek said. "My electrons are not spin-paired. And don't be so sure of yourself. You're not ferromagnetic either. If our subshells were completely filled with electrons then we wouldn't be able to affect each other as much. But we do. We are just normal paramagnets. Take us away from each other and we may lose our power, put us together and we may push and pull, attract and repel, but we're not diamagnetic and I don't know about you, but I think there's some kind of external magnetic field here that helps us become magnetic."

Matt laughed. "Wow. Okay. Well, um, more power to you both. I will be in here with the humans."

I smiled. "You know your chemistry."

He nodded. "I know chemistry when I see it."

Chapter Six
Derek

Maybe my magnetism speech convinced her to be spontaneous with me, whatever the case we ended up at her apartment after the party. I sat on her bed and watched her pack twenty six shirts, fifteen pants, eight shorts, six skirts, forty two dresses, eleven leggings and tights, nineteen pairs of shoes, six bottles of hair dye, a ton of jewelry, and an entire suitcase devoted to makeup and hair products. I didn't say a word. Smiled, nodded, and placed her seven luggage contraptions next to my solitary backpack filled with one brown shirt, a pair of pants, my bathing suit, a toothbrush, and one clean pair of underwear.

She sat in the passengers seat and exhaled. I shut her door, sat down beside her, and said, "You do realize we are only going to be gone a week, right?"

"I like to be prepared."

Understatement of the century.

We drove a while until we hit tons of traffic, so we decided to stop and get something to eat. GPS led us to a Red Lobster in Maryland. We ordered, blinked at each other, and ate.

"You haven't said a word since we left." She smoothed her lime hair into a pony tail. "Where are we going anyway?"

"A cruise."

"Are you serious? That's one of my biggest fears."

"A cruise?"

"Um, yes. Remember Titantic?"

I laughed. "Well, we're not going on a ship so don't worry."

"Do you have any fears?"

"Heights."

"Heights? As in airplanes or ladders?"

"Both."

"Tell me why you want me to do this."

"Because we both need a vacation and you happen to be my closest friend right now."

"More like your only friend."

"Pretty much."

"Unlike you to be so agreeable."

"Unlike you to be so sarcastic."

She smiled.

"So, you ready?" I said.

"No." She put her elbows on the table and leaned forward. "Not until you answer a question for me."

"Depends on the question."

"It can't. You have to answer or I'm not getting back in your car."

"What if I picked you up and tied you down?"

"Kinky, huh?"

"Do you flirt with everyone or do I get special treatment?"

She hesitated. Unsure of which answer would upset me the most. I gave the waitress my card and watched Miranda put her hair down again and braid it.

"Do you ever sit still?" I said.

She straightened her shoulders, closed her eyes like someone about to do a yoga session, and stayed like that until the waitress set the check on the table. Miranda popped up and snorted like a pig on steroids. The waitress jumped and knocked over a glass of water, then walked away in a huff.

"What the hell was that?" I said as I signed the bill and gave the girl a fifty dollar tip. "I'm starting to think twice here." I shook my head. Her child-like spirit refreshed the dying parts of me. After living alone in a desert at the bottom of an empty well, I needed a drink. Too many years hiding. Too many years wasted. Her stubborn pride annoyed me, but the more time I spent with her the more I remembered life before David Bennett stole the very breath from my lungs.

"You gonna answer my question or what?" she said, with no intentions of giving up.

"Sure."

"Why did you go off to college and not even tell your family what you were doing?"

"How do you know that?"

"Ella said you never told anyone where you went. Just disappeared."

"Honestly?"

She nodded.

"The tip of that iceberg is simple. I was ashamed."

For the first time since I met Miranda, that brisk autumn day when my sister got married in a field, we held eye contact for longer than two seconds. She analyzed my eyes for clues as I admired the flecks of gold stretching across hers. We didn't stop staring into each other until an old man fell beside our table. His cane hit my leg and Miranda knelt beside him before I even realized what happened.

I checked his pulse, then pressed my ear against his nose. His chest stopped moving and I felt no breath on my skin. Pulse non-existent. "Miranda," I said. "Go to my car and grab the little red lunchbox-looking thing from under the passengers seat."

She jogged off as I pressed my palm into his chest and shoved my body weight into the poor man. After thirty chest compressions I positioned his head, pinched his nose, and exhaled a gentle puff of air into his mouth, then started compressions again. Miranda returned and dropped the AED on the floor beside me. I took it out, bypassed the promptings, and gave Miranda scissors. "Cut his shirt down the middle." I motioned to everyone hovered around. "Please move back. I need everyone to take a step back." I took off my button-down shirt and wiped his chest dry, then placed two pads on him and attached the cables. A young woman, maybe the man's daughter, gripped his hand. "Ma'am please step back. I can't have you touch him right now." She listened as I pressed the button allowing the AED to analyze the heart rhythm. Once it finished I told everyone to stand back again and I pressed the orange button to activate the shock. Back to compressions.

Sirens blasted through the restaurant. People cleared a path for the EMS. I delivered a quick speech. Told them what I did. Patient slightly responsive. Then I grabbed the AED and walked to my car. Fast. Completely unaware that I had forgotten Miranda until she sat in the car beside me, shut the door, and put her hands in her lap.

I turned the keys in the ignition, watched the man's stretcher-cradled body slip into the back of the ambulance. Had been a while since I'd done that. Something about it felt ... almost ... wrong.

Miranda's hand cut through the summer wind as she put her blue toe-nails on the dashboard, tilted her head back, and closed her eyes. The sun glistened on her cheeks as I veered back onto the highway, inhaled deeply, and shifted into third gear. With the click of a button the sunroof opened, casting warmth on our faces. Miranda opened her eyes. Looked at me. Smiled.

I looked away, afraid of what I might find if I stared too long in her direction. She opened the glove compartment and rummaged through the envelopes. All hundred and seven of them.

"Any pens in here?" she said.

I shook my head.

"What are all the envelopes? Letters from a lover?"

"No. They aren't letters."

She held one up to the sunroof. "Can I open it?"

"Is it yours?"

She shrugged and put it back with the others. "You're weird."

I laughed. "I'm weird?"

"Why is everything a mystery with you?"

"Everything is a mystery to the one who doesn't understand."

I pulled off the highway and drove to the nearest street light.

"Pick a direction," I said. "Right, left, or straight."

She perked up like a flower kissed by the sun. "Really?"

I nodded and she pointed to the right. I let her choose at the next four stop lights until we found our way to a road dotted with suburban houses and SUVs. I parked and looked around.

"Pick a house," I said. "Any house."

She pointed to the one with missing shutters and overgrown grass. The only one with rose bushes that hadn't bloomed and a swing set that had seen one too many days. The exact house I would've chosen.

"Take one of those envelopes and put it in the mailbox," I said.

She followed my directions and sat back down. "You're definitely weird, but I like this side of you."

"What made you choose that house?"

"It has character and hope. The mark of a life well-lived."

"Really? Is that what you see?"

"What do you see?"

"Unpaid bills, one too many kids, and a strained marriage."

The lines on her forehead wrinkled and creased. "I see a family who would rather cook dinner together than plant flowers. A mother more consumed with loving her kids than cleaning her house. A life well-lived, albeit not as clean as the life next door."

"Do you see everything with a nice pink bow on top?"

She pointed to the immaculate house next door. Three pristine cars parked outside with shiny wheels. A garden bursting with color. Freshly painted bricks. New roof. Trimmed grass. And a man kneeling to pick up a newspaper as he walked from his car to the house, careful not to dirty his three-piece suit.

"There," she said.

"What?"

"There I see a strained marriage, one too many bills, and not enough children."

"What would you consider enough children?"

"Enough to make you less absorbed in yourself, your money, your hobbies, possessions, you name it."

"What about people who have ten kids but still care more about blogging their lives away than they do living them?"

"I don't know. I guess some people are so deep into themselves that they can't see it anymore. Maybe they believe they're altruistic when really their entire concept of reality is guided by their false perception of the world around them."

I shifted gears and drove back to the highway. Miranda Ryan. Never met a girl like her. Ever. Strange as they come, but underneath that hair she was intelligent, alarmingly profound, and beautiful. More beautiful than any woman I'd ever known. More intriguing too.

She saw life through Miranda-colored glasses. And I'm certain those glasses were a one-of-a-kind pair. Worth more than a thousand green Ben Franklin's.

Chapter Seven
Miranda

The Derek Rhodes story kept getting more and more interesting. I found myself flipping through pages with excitement, wanting to unearth the hidden passages of his heart. Then the envelopes. There were hundreds of them, or so it seemed, piled inside his glove compartment. Hundreds. And he chose random houses as the recipients of these mysterious letters.

I couldn't stop thinking about them during the entire drive to the destination, which, by the way, I still didn't know a thing about. The boring brown shirt man was mysterious. I liked that. I liked him more and more by the second.

After another gas station stop and a long stretch of driving, he finally parked at what seemed to be a fishing center. I looked around, wondering if he planned to buy fishing gear before the trip, but he opened the trunk and began putting my luggage into a somewhat small boat. At least small compared to a cruise ship, but bigger than some of the boats lined up beside it.

"This is Nettle," he said, tapping the side of the boat as it rocked in the green water. "My boat and our ride to the place we'll be staying."

I pushed the side and watched the boat sway amidst plastic bottles and trash piled up by the dock. Perhaps he saw the concern on my face. I'm not good at hiding my true colors. Well, unless you count my hair. He squeezed my shoulder and said, "It's safe."

I wasn't so sure, but I pretended to be. He finished tossing our stuff into the boat and held my hand as I leaped from the sturdy peer to the not-so-sturdy boat. I adored science. Completely aware of density and the mechanics of floating boats in murky water, but still ... little boats in deep water didn't tickle my fancy. If I weren't so bent on figuring out Derek and seeing him break out of his shell I wouldn't have gotten in the car, much less the boat. The rocking, unsteady, teeny boat with no roof.

I sat down, hoping that when he turned the thing on I'd stay in the boat and not fly off the side. Not that I couldn't swim, just that I imagined myself flying off, hitting the motor, and bleeding to death at the bottom of the water. And which water was it anyway? An inlet from the Atlantic? A river? A reservoir? I didn't ask. Just like I didn't ask why Derek had a heart attack shock thing in his car, or how he knew exactly what do to when that man fell, or the way he talked with the ambulance people like he knew more than they did, and most especially, why he had a bunch of blank envelopes in his car that he put in random mailboxes.

I didn't ask. Although my mind dreamed of a trillion possibilities. A trillion, I tell ya. Stories swirled inside my brain and painted my heart with wild colors. Who could Derek really be? Perhaps someone more exciting than brown shirts and sarcasm galore. And where could he be taking me? An exotic resort filled with possibilities of life beyond the mundane?

I held on to the bar beside me as he did something that made the engine roar into the air like a bear at the top of a mountain. I could practically see the sound rippling across the water. I didn't realize he untied the boat and pushed us further into the gross-looking water. Why did people trash the world? I never understood that. What does it take to put your soda bottle in a trash can? I could totally see Michael Jackson in my head. Arms outstretched. Fire blazing behind him as he half-angrily, but with so much passion, screamed to all of us, "Do you ever stop to notice this crying earth, this weeping shore?"

I reached for my phone in my purse. After a few minutes of searching to no avail, Derek finally handed it to me. "Looking for this?"

I tried to turn it on. Nothing. After a few seconds of waiting for it to light up, I checked the battery. It was missing.

Derek smiled. "I took the battery out."

"Why? Can I have it?"

"No." He stopped the motor thingy and stood. "And now it's time to shed your addictions."

"What are you talking about?"

"You might hate me for this, but one day you might love me for it. So,

38

for your sake, I'm willing to take the chance."

"Seriously, you are getting more and more bizarre by the minute."

"Takes a very skilled one to know one."

I tried to laugh. Truth is, he worried me. Purely because I had no idea what on earth he meant. Then, he lifted my luggage and tossed every last one into the water. Completely shocked, I watched my suitcases float back to Michael Jackson as Derek revved the boat up and floored it toward the land ahead of us. Then it sunk in. Deep in. Deep into a part of me I didn't know existed. A part of me that wanted to jump into the water and float with my clothes to my death, to their death, because for whatever reason losing all of my favorite outfits felt like losing my soul. I slouched into the boat and pretended not to care. Inside I fought the urge to sink my teeth into his flesh. Who did he think he was? And what did he think I was? A project? A Cinderella in need of saving?

No. I likened myself to Mulan. Maybe Pochantas. Eowyn in Lord of the Rings. Not Jenny in Forrest Gump. Or darling Cinderelli locked in the basement with nothing to do except hope for someone to discover that the shoe fits. That was not me. Why did he think that was me?

I didn't speak to him. He anchored his boat once we reached land. No man's land. Avoiding Derek and his gaze, I jumped to shore and looked around, wondering how long he planned to stay until going to the resort, but a few minutes later I watched as he pushed the boat and stood with his hands in his pockets as it drifted away and turned into a tiny circle atop smooth waves. He pulled a plastic bag from his backpack and handed it to me.

I snatched it and looked inside. An antique-ish looking Victorian night gown. A journal. And a pack of pens. Blue ink. Fine tip.

"Is this some kind of joke?" I said.

"What do you think of our resort?" He smiled.

"Am I supposed to sleep in the wilderness?"

"You said you wanted me to live a little."

"I guess we have different views of life."

"I guess so." He pointed behind him. "There's a place I go to up there. I've got some camp gear to set up."

I didn't want to give him the pleasure of knowing how much he made me want to throw sand and rocks at his face, so I smiled and pretended not to be bothered by his annoying plans. I'm not a girly girl by any means, but this was not my idea of vacation. And he had the audacity to take my phone battery. If he weren't Ella's brother I would've feared for my life.

He hiked up some hill while I sat in the spot he left me. Light waves lapped against the rocky shore. Not crystal clear water against a white beach. More like bay water against rocks with a tad bit of sand for good measure. I sighed and watched the sun show off before taking its bow.

I picked up my journal and the one Derek bought. His voice surprised me. I stood and turned around, one journal in each hand.

"Ready for s'mores?" he said.

I looked at the journals. My hand yearned for the pen like most girls pined over men. The feeling of smooth ink grazing some sort of parchment, curving into letters and words and sentences. Paragraphs of life and passion.

He pointed to my hands. "Pick one."

"Pick what?"

"A journal. Right now you need to choose. That journal in your right hand holds your past. This one"—he pointed to the spiral bound college-ruled aquamarine notebook he bought—"is a clean slate. So, keep writing a continuation of your past in that fine-leather journal or toss it into the water and start with a blank page."

I didn't like either option. So I tucked both into my bag and followed him up the hill. We walked over sticks, through dirt, around rocks, under fallen trees, and it was during that walk that I realized why Derek must've liked brown so much. Boring like some old woods in the middle of nowhere. Dirt, sticks, and some occasional green plants and grass.

He stopped in front of some kind of entrance hidden by long green vines, pulled the vines toward us, and ushered me inside. I ducked and climbed between two moss-covered tree trunks and gasped when I reached the other side.

"This is my getaway." Derek climbed in and stood beside me. "What do you think?"

How could I think? I couldn't believe it. A small tent in the middle of countless flowers of every color. Ivy growing tall, choking the necks of trees. Wisteria floated above my head, dangling in rows of white and purple and sparkling in the sunlight. I brushed them with my hands as I glanced at the wild roses. Pink and white from what I could see. Right behind them a river of blue flowers winded its way through red, orange, and green. To the left of the tent a small charcoal grill and three fishing rods sat on top of a brick circle. Birds chirped above us, obviously delighted by the colorful blend of life beneath them. Lots of color. Lots of life. Lots of dedication to make that tiny nook so special. I looked at Derek. Hands in his pockets, he leaned back on his heels. He was proud of this place and by the charm in his eyes I could tell it meant a lot to him. I saw a glimmer of the child inside and it softened my frustration with him. For now, at least.

I grabbed his arm and looked around in a panic. "Where's Auntie Em?"

He smiled. "You're the only person that's been here with me. I've never shown it to anyone."

"Really? How long have you been coming here?"

"A few years." He handed me a bag. "Graham crackers, marshmallows, and chocolate. I'll get the fire going."

He lit a fire and knelt beside it. His arms and face glowed in the flickering light as he placed a few more sticks into the flames. For the life of me, I tried not to stare too much at him, but I'd never seen him so lit up before. And it wasn't just the fire.

Then it hit me. I'd never been camping before. Bugs, snakes, sleeping on the ground with only fabric between me and the wilderness.

"I'm sorry about the clothes," he said.

I nodded, handed him a marshmallow, and avoided his apology.

"Look." He tossed a stick my way. "I have some money. Once we leave I'll take you shopping and you can buy thousands of dollars worth of clothes."

"Thousands?" I laughed. "Living in dreamland today?"

"Those envelopes each have five-hundred dollars in them. I keep them in my car and give them to random strangers. A single mom frazzled in the grocery line because her card is denied. A hard working dad who can't afford a water heater. A kid in the wrong neighborhood who is tempted to sell drugs to buy a nice pair of shoes. Random houses that look like they could use some help." He stuffed his marshmallow on a stick. "Not saying

41

this to get some kind of compliment. Just saying I have money. Plenty of it. And I have no intentions of spending it on myself."

"Why do you have so much money?"

"Good at saving, I guess."

"What did you do for a living?"

He closed his eyes and sucked in a lot of air, then let it go.

"What's wrong?"

"Nothing," he said. "Just something about that word. Living."

I shrugged and put my marshmallow into the fire beside his. "You know roasting marshmallows is an art, right?"

"Everything is an art to you."

I smiled. "You want to hold it a little higher than the fire. Not right in the flames. Then turn it real slow like this." I twisted the stick. "That way it cooks evenly all throughout. At the end, it will be super gooey inside and crunchy outside. Delicious, I tell ya." I pretended not to notice his sudden expression of doom and figured I'd change the subject back to me. "So why'd you do that to my clothes?"

"I can tell you're a lot like me," he said. "I hide behind a boring life and you hide behind a colorful life, but fact is, we're both hiding."

"I'm not hiding from anything. This is just who I am."

He looked into my eyes and held contact until I glanced down.

"You are beautiful," he said. "The green hair doesn't flatter your natural beauty."

"You don't understand me." I sandwiched my marshmallow between the chocolate and graham crackers. "I'm not trying to be a natural beauty. I'm just doing what I enjoy." I took a bite and waited for him to have some sort of sarcastic response, but he didn't. "Some guys happen to think green hair is more beautiful than the normal colors, you know."

"Yes. Something I can't fathom."

"One of the many reasons I can't fathom being with you."

He didn't flinch. Not even the slightest hint of irritation. Surprising. Actually made me feel bad for saying it. Normally he bantered with me, almost in a playful way.

"Sorry," I said.

He nodded, telling me with his eyes that it was okay, but his mind

42

remained somewhere else. Some distant place. A place I wanted to know. "What do my clothes have to do with hiding, anyway?"

"Just thought it would help you."

"How?"

"Sometimes we don't realize we're drowning." His shoulders dropped as he spread his legs out in front of him. A thin veil of melancholy colored his face. "Sometimes we need someone to help us see the chains stuck to our feet. All these chains." He breathed deep. "They keep us from swimming back to oxygen. Maybe I was wrong, maybe you don't do all of this because you're like me. Maybe you're better. Maybe you're strong, fun, happy." He rubbed his clean-shaven face. "Maybe I'm the negative one who sees everything the wrong way, but I figured we all have something keeping us away from real life. Some sort of temptation to drown in a river and rot at the bottom. I assumed that clothes and hair and all this pointless stuff"—he waved his hand up and down me—"was the stuff you hide behind. The stuff that keeps you from facing reality, but I'm willing to admit that I'm wrong."

I stared through the fire. To the tree behind it, surrounded by flowers. The light casted a beautiful golden hue on everything around us, including his face. I looked back to the tree and thought of the seed I planted in the backyard with my brother. We watered the seed every day together. Every day until I became a teenager and made the biggest mistake of my life. The one thing I regret more than anything else. Poor Max. I'll never forget his face. Every day he watered the seed, but it never grew. He still watered the exact spot every day after. Couldn't speak. Couldn't even go on the potty. But he believed that if he kept watering and shining his flashlight on that mound of dirt, that a tree would grow. I didn't have the heart to tell him it wouldn't. I didn't have a heart at all, really. It died the day I chose popularity over love.

Maybe Derek was right about me, but I didn't see chains. All I wanted was to be someone different. Someone I wanted to be. I spent way too much of my life trying to please others and failing myself in the process, but maybe I leaned on my clothes too much. And all those bottles of hair dye. Who am I? I wondered, not entirely happy that he caused me to wonder. I pulled the two journals out of my purse and pondered which one to use.

"Well," I said. "Blank pages or the pages I've always known."

Derek looked up.

I stuffed my worn journal into my bag and opened to the first page of the blank spiral-bound. A blank page. A new world waiting to be unraveled in letters. I waited, thought for a minute, then pressed my pen to the paper. Here goes....

Chapter Eight
Derek

It's more likely that people will forever deny who they really are than go on the dark and lonely battle of discovering the places they fear, the places tucked inside their soul that even they have yet to meet. I knew that. Knew it well. I avoided myself like Pinocchio avoided the truth. And whether Miranda wanted to admit it or not, something caused her to become attached to her persona. Or should I say lack of persona. Various Madonna-like reinventions. But never really truly herself. I wanted to help her and I knew my motivations weren't selfless. I thought if I helped her see the light maybe I'd find it too. Saving her would save me.

But she had more stubborn fuel than a cowboys untamed horse. No breaking her in. If so, she didn't let on. I hadn't seen her so quiet until I introduced her to my little corner of the earth. I liked seeing her think and process things, but she never shared her thoughts. Only when she felt sorry for me. At least it seemed that way.

She tucked herself under the blankets and curled up into fetal position. I zipped up the tent and said, "Goodnight."

"You're not sleeping in here?"

"It's all yours."

She unzipped and looked at me. "But I'm a little worried about bugs and snakes and stuff."

"That's why you're in the tent and I'm out here."

"But what if they climb inside?"

"Just sleep. If a snake comes I will be attacked before you."

She laughed. "How reassuring."

"Get some sleep."

"I guess I can try."

She zipped the tent back up and rustled inside. I rolled up a few clumps of weeds and formed a pillow, then stared at the strands of wisteria hanging above me. No stars. Just wisteria glistening in flakes of moonlight. Every plant around me had meaning. One day I hoped for the courage to tell someone. Maybe Miranda. Someone who wouldn't shriek and run off. Not sure how anyone could love me if I didn't love myself, but the heart can only take so much loneliness before it wilts up and dies.

Alone.

I wondered how the old man was doing. Seemed like he'd be okay, but you never know how the heart will jump back to life after trauma like that. I sometimes wondered what would be more painful. Dying of a broken heart emotionally or physically. After experiencing the emotional I think I'd take the physical brokenness.

I imagined my heart spread all over the place. So many shredded remnants of a once-beating organ.

Shredded.

The images haunted me. I could barely sleep most nights without waking up in horror. The nightmare that I was David Bennett again. A horrible, heartless man so cold and far from love.

A man I never imagined becoming and now I couldn't forget. And I tried like you wouldn't believe. Things like that don't walk out of your life. They're tattooed so deep in the skin you'll never be able to get rid of them.

A cool breeze swept across me and carried his name on its wings.

Owen.

At least that's what I imagined his name to be. I fell asleep with his name on my mind and woke up when I dreamt of Ashleigh's final threats. The pattern repeated until daybreak when Miranda's sleepy eyes looked at me with gentleness. I never imagined spending so much time with someone like her. My friends were so different. Ashleigh was a thousand times the opposite of Miranda. My entire life was something Miranda would've despised. Just like I did. Underneath. Took me too long to realize it. Too many mistakes later.

"You slept on weeds?" she said as she stretched her arms and back.

I nodded, trying not to notice her curves.

"So. How long are we staying here and what are we going to do?"

"I didn't plan that far ahead." I sat up. "Can't believe your not pissed at me for sailing your wardrobe away."

She raised her eyebrows. "Who said I'm not?"

"My ex would've been throwing stuff and trying to rip my hair out. Are you more internal or something?"

"Your ex sounds nice." She looked around. "What's for breakfast?"

I walked to the tent, grabbed my bag, and handed her a carton of eggs. She shrugged her shoulders, looking for the kitchen. I laughed and opened the grill to reveal a cast iron skillet underneath.

"You want me to cook eggs on that?" she said. "Looks gross."

"I've seen you put gum in your mouth after it fell on the pavement and you're worried about a cast iron skillet?"

"Well, how do I start the grill?"

"I will." I lit a fire and took the eggs. "And I will even cook for you."

She reached for the coconut oil by the grill. "Can I use some of this on my hair?"

"Your hair?"

"My hair."

I handed it to her and watched her lather a small amount in her hands, then rub it into the ends of her hair. She looked at me with that "what?" look in her eyes. Minding my own business, I focused on the eggs. When I finished frying them I gave her three on a paper plate. She took the plate, mouthed "thank you," and slipped out of the wisteria haven. A few minutes later she came back with the empty plate.

"Looks like it might rain," she said. "You have a mosquito on your arm."

I looked down and blew it away. It came back immediately, this time on my hand. I blew it away again.

"You know it's going to keep coming back unless you kill it, right?"

I winced and turned my face from her eyes. She followed me in a circle, forcing our eyes to meet. I sat down.

"You alright?" she said, scooting close to me.

I nodded as another mosquito landed on my arm. She raised her arm. I jerked away. She slapped my knee instead.

"Are you okay?" Some sliver of gentleness washed over her tone. Her entire body actually. She squeezed my hand as I held back anger. Tear-soaked anger. Blood-soaked anger. David Bennett. I hated him. Despised him with every bit of passion in me. And he was me. "He was me."

"Who was?" Her sweet voice carried me back from the storm. Back to Derek Rhodes. The man I couldn't figure out how to be. The man I wished to be, but how? After everything I did? When I looked in the mirror I saw David Bennett, which is why I didn't look into them until my hair and beard made him disappear.

"Okay, so you brought me to a strange island thing and tossed my clothes into the abyss. You wanted to know why I wasn't cracking your skull open with the cast-iron after such things. Well, here goes." She squeezed my hand again, let go, and stood. "My dad was never the kind of dad who sat his little girl on his lap. I'm the only girl out of four boys. So you'd think maybe the man would've had some kind of soft spot for a little girl with pig tails and big eyes." She paced as she spoke so fast I could barely take it all in. "I can't tell you how many times I wanted to sit on his lap and read a story. Or just sit there. He pushed me away when I tried to. Said his legs hurt. My butt was too bony. He was tired. My head blocked the television. He couldn't reach the remote. Endless excuses. So I tried to get his attention. I tried to twirl around and dance in front of the television. He didn't like that, so I assumed he didn't like dance. Well, he must like what's always on the television. Football. So I collected football cards, played sports with the boys, had absolutely no girl friends, and immersed myself in boydom. Hoping maybe he'd come outside and play catch with me or watch me score the winning touch down because no boy could keep up with my fast sprint. Let's just say he never came outside. He never noticed me. So I shifted my attention to kids at school. I tried to be popular. Changed my hair. Changed my clothes. Changed my taste in movies, music, you name it, all for the sake of having someone, somewhere notice me."

She exhaled and looked at me. I didn't know what to say. I didn't know how to heal hearts. Only how to break them.

"I made the biggest and worst decision of my life because of my desire to be popular and the person I need forgiveness from can't speak." She tried to hold herself together, but I could see that her glue was pretty weak. "So, the reason, I guess, I've been so into changing my appearance is because for once in my life I am doing whatever I want to do in that moment."

I cleared my throat and chose my words with caution. "Please grab the cast-iron if what I'm about to say offends you."

She smiled and sat beside me. Her shoulder touched mine and sent a shiver down my arms. A girl's touch hadn't had that effect on me since tenth grade.

"So?" she said.

"So ... your dad obviously had some issues, but why let that define who you are today?"

"I'm not. That's my point. I do all of this for myself. To be what I want and not what everyone else wants."

"I don't believe it." This time I squeezed her hand. "If you weren't seeking approval from others you wouldn't get so upset when I challenged the things you do and like."

She stared at our hands. I did too. In a strange silent moment that could've been romantic had she not been on the verge of an emotional meltdown or breakthrough and I have to admit, I was a little worried it would be a meltdown.

"When I saw those clothes float away I wasn't angry," she said. "I was scared. An odd depressed feeling. Maybe that turned into a protest against you and what you did, but mostly because I don't know who I am without that stuff. It's like the person I am is many people and without all of those people I'm nothing."

"So you live in a constant state of rebellion. Now you don't even know what the hell you're rebelling against, do you?"

"I didn't even know I was rebelling."

"Your dad didn't notice you, so you sought it at school. I'm assuming you've had your heart broken and each time you rebelled against that particular Miranda in hopes of finding a version of you that people liked. Right now you are rebelling against it all. You didn't find what you were looking for so you gave up and instead of looking inward to find out who you really are, you reverted back to outward expression to rebel against the old you."

"Wow. Pretty fly for a white guy."

"Am I right?" I breathed in. "I know I am because I have the same illness. I just go into hiding."

"Awww. It's like you're a turtle and I'm a lizard."

"Huh?"

"The Adventures of Turtle and Lizzy." She laughed. "You hide in your shell and I hide by changing my colors."

I couldn't help but laugh, and that means she succeeded in something no person ever had before. "You are the first person who has ever made me laugh when it was the absolute last thing I wanted to do."

Chapter Nine
Miranda

Derek and I reclined against a tree and talked until drops of rain landed on our noses. We shifted gears and spoke of childhood memories and favorite movies. Not the deep stuff. Not the painful images my heart wanted to forget. I wanted to tell him everything. Right there in the middle of nowhere. No one to hear. No one besides him. I didn't trust anyone with my heart. Not after every relationship I pursued ended up an unrequited love story. Only two people knew my regret. Matt and Gavin. I spilled my heart to them a year after it happened. They were older. Wiser. And I needed to vent. Gavin told me to tell Max that I was sorry and allow myself to move on. Matt repeated. And I obeyed. Trouble is, Autism speaks in ways I didn't understand. Max couldn't give me forgiveness. He couldn't tell me he was okay. He couldn't tell me that I didn't crush his dreams and that he really, really was okay.

He didn't have a voice.

"You alright?" Derek cracked my memories and peeled back reality. "You look deep in thought."

"You're not telling me everything," I said. "And I won't force you, because I want you to come to the point I'm at now."

He shifted his weight to the left and pulled his knee to his chest, then raked his head where his former hair used to be.

I continued, "I trust you."

He avoided my eyes.

I looked down too. "I've trusted few people with my heart, so tread lightly. I told you my brother Max and I wanted to plant something together, but we never did. See"—I steadied myself on a low tree branch—"I wanted to fit in. I was the type of girl who sat at pep rally's and high school

51

football games pining over boys who never knew my name. I wrote poems about them. Cried in my car to Radiohead's Creep about them. I practiced writing my name with their last names. Knew their class schedule by heart and where they stood before the bells rang." I stopped, inhaled as much air as possible, and looked at the grey clouds before I continued. "Finally, my chance had come. I did something dumb. I called this guy randomly from my friends house, blocked my number, and told him I wouldn't reveal my identity until he guessed who I was. I'd call him every night at eight and give him one clue each night. To my surprise, he loved our conversations and seemed as excited as I was. Then one day I messed up. I was relaying a story and accidentally said my name. A few nights later he figured out my identity. It was so awkward after that. He stopped calling. I thought we'd fall in love and it would be magical. The unknown girl gets the popular guy. The Taylor Swift song comes to life."

"So, then what?"

"He called me one night. I almost had a heart attack. He knew who I was and still called me. A few minutes into the conversation he told me about this beautiful girl he liked and asked my advice for how to approach her. My heart probably stopped beating as I told him what a girl would like. Anyway, long story short, he ended up with her and I got depressed. That soon turned into a determination to become so beautiful and popular that he would regret his decision. So I had a bit of a transformation and showed up at school one day. No one recognized me. I felt so high on life. All the guys turned their heads. And by the end of the week I was drinking with the cool kids, who, turned out to be not as cool as I imagined."

"Did he regret his decision?"

"Who knows, but I got so into my new status that I made the biggest regret of my life. Well, several of them, including marijuana episodes, but there's one that I just can't forget.

"My little brother was outside one morning. I was a junior in high school and loving life. He was watering the grass in the front yard when I pulled up and got out of my car. He liked watering plants and grass. He'd just stare at the stream of water for hours if we let him. He was really young at the time and I had already started ignoring him to be with my friends. When I got out of the car my brother started jumping up and down and

52

making all kinda of weird sounds. Cool guy that I had a crush on pulled up to my house. Asked if I lived there. I said, 'No,' embarrassed of Max. He got out of the car and asked me out on a date. Then he started jumping up and down making fun of Max. I was worried he wouldn't believe my lie if I didn't make fun of Max too. So I did."

"This isn't that bad, Miranda." He seemed so sure. So sure of all my uncertainties. "It's nothing compared to what I did."

"I've barely talked to Max since." Tears dripped from my eyes, meddling with the rain. "He closed up, Derek. Even more than he was before. His counselor was just starting to get somewhere with him. Then he shut down. I'll never forget his face that day. The hose fell to the ground, spraying him in the face. He panicked because he doesn't like getting wet. I walked away, laughing and hiding my broken heart." My voice rose and fell as I spoke with my fists clenched into balls. "Laughing. I laughed at him as he had a meltdown. My mom heard him and came outside but I was already driving away. All for what? For some guy who wanted to screw me. That's it. Not even passionate love-making. He wanted to use my body and our conversations gave him a doorway into my pants. At least I wasn't that stupid. Just stupid enough to hurt the sweetest kid in the world."

Derek stood in front of me and held my arms. I shoved the tears to a faraway land and looked into his eyes. The rain picked up, but we stayed there, staring at each other as the summer sky darkened. He ran his fingertips up and down my arms, then stopped on my hands. Rain tapped hard on the leaves around us. A rhythmic pulse. I bared my soul, my deepest regrets, and all I could think about was how bad I wanted him to kiss me. He leaned toward me. Pressed his body into mine and held me like a husband holds his wife. I consented. Allowing our bodies to touch when our lips couldn't. For years I used guys as an escape from myself. My pain. My past. A kiss is all it took to send me into the stars, bouncing off the glowing fire balls from one romance to another. If you could call it romance.

Derek pulled back, his shirt soaked and clinging to his obviously defined chest. I looked up, allowing the rain to land on my eyelids, my cheeks, my neck. And I inhaled the life around me.

"My regrets are five-thousand and seventy times worse," he said.

A deep cry immersed from my heart. Then another. But he couldn't tell. Our bodies were laden with the earths tears. Mine blended in. The tears I should've cried long ago. Instead of smiling as my brother screamed in the yard, wondering why his best friend made fun of him.

Derek's palm rested against my cheek. I placed my hand over top of his. The weight of the wind bore down on the trees as they crouched and swung in the howling sky. Throned in sheets of lightening, somber clouds hovered, taunting us. It wasn't the wrestling sky that scared me. Or the fleeting thought of Dorothy carried in a breeze. It was the feeling I had, as the sea and the air became one, that perhaps I loved the man in front of me. Perhaps the warmth of his hand really was making me forget I was wet and cold. And scared.

The storm hissed and wailed as Derek pulled me back to his garden. He shoved some bricks into the tent and pushed me inside, then followed after. We sat together. His body next to mine, close enough to feel his arm muscles move, but too far to hear him breathe. The night, alive and well, entertained us with its exploding thunder and etches of light.

I didn't fear the man sitting beside me.

I feared my inability to give my heart fully, unadulterated, and guiltlessly to another soul. And no, it wasn't the giving that petrified me. It was the *forever* that would bind my soul to another's. That intimidated me even more than the crashing trees around us.

Derek inched toward me and cupped my face. "You okay?"

"Yes," I said, but he couldn't hear me over the whipping and lashing of nature.

Lightening streaked the sky, imprinting shadows of trees on the fabric around us. I thought of Max and I huddled under blankets when we made shadow stories with our hands. I begged my parents for another sibling. I wanted a sister so bad. All boys. And I didn't want to be the baby. Dad didn't want another kid. Not sure he even wanted the ones he had.

Max was an accident.

When emotional storms swept through our house at night, they didn't know I was listening. So many times I heard my father whisper in a tone so fierce it made me cringe, "One night of pleasure wasn't worth a lifetime of autism." My mother's sobs climbed three flights of stairs and smoothed their way under the crack beneath my door. I'd creep into Max's room and thankfully find him asleep, in peace, unaware of how unwanted he was.

I could relate.

Until I spoke the same lie into his heart that my father spoke into all of his children.

You are not worth the love of another.

Holding Max all those nights I told myself over and over, "Tuck your heart away, Miranda. Tuck it away and don't let anyone in." Now, after all those years of tucking away, my world was being changed by the man who only wore brown.

Stranger things have happened, I suppose.

Chapter Ten
Derek

I held her until she fell asleep. The storm settled as she rested in my hands. I couldn't believe it. She opened up and gave me a piece of herself and by the uncontrollable tears, I had a feeling I was the first guy besides her brother and brother-from-another-mother that ever saw her cry. Her regrets may not have been half as repulsive as mine, but you always feel like your scars are the deepest because they're your own. Pain isn't comparable. My measuring stick doesn't work for anyone else but me. Which is why I've never been a fan of the "suck it up" mentality.

I watched her sleep as long as I could. Wanting to rub her face, but afraid she wouldn't like it. She rustled a few times and her hair fell, like a blanket over her eyes. I moved the fading green strands of hair behind her shoulder and zeroed in on her lips. Slightly open. Relaxed. Looking quite kissable.

Women are off limits, I reminded myself. They brought nothing but problems.

I rolled onto my back and listened to the slight tap of rain. Probably falling from the thirsty wisteria vines above us. Miranda was a quiet and still sleeper. Not like Ashleigh. That girl always stole the covers and snored louder than most men I knew. She was gorgeous. Although her personality quickly made her the ugliest person I'd ever known. Funny how the most beautiful people in the world aren't always the types to gloss the covers of magazines and yet most people spend their lives trying to turn heads.

David Bennett knew all about arrogant and attention-seeking pride. I could see it so clear. Images of my former self, trying to be cool, and succeeding, only to regret every moment I lived without my heart. Fun, sure. But not authentic. Life without the heart is cold and lonely, no matter how many people fill your apartment.

I spent too much of my life like a thanksgiving turkey. Filled to the brim, but dead.

Miranda moved closer to me. I turned my head. Such beauty staring back at me. A woman in the middle of the night. Something about it could ruin me if I let it. All inhibitions are gone in the middle of the night. Or is it just me? I had a tendency to bare my soul when the lights went down. Especially tempting with her. The way she looked right now. Stripped from all of her masks. Vulnerable and real. A real woman. I don't think I'd ever been so close to something so beautiful.

She touched my arm. "Derek?"

I nodded.

She sat up and traced my brow with her hand, then ran her fingers through my hair. I tried not to look at her. I'm not known for my self-control and she was pushing buttons I didn't know I had. I loved her eyes. They changed depending on the colors she wore. Or her hair color. Right now they looked grey.

"Why so serious?" I said.

"Do you think I'm pretty?" This wasn't a question. It was a need. When I didn't answer she pressed her fingers against the tips of mine and said, "Because you seem like you're just trying to change who I am. Like every other guy I've ever known."

I ignored the physical sensations as her hand touched mine. "I'm not trying to change you. Blue, pink, brown hair. Doesn't matter much to me. I'm trying to help you find out who Miranda really is. Not the version of you that depends on what other people like. And definitely not the version that rebels against what other people like. Just you."

"So." She pulled a damp piece of hair in front of her face and held it there. "Do you think I'm pretty?"

I closed my eyes. "Doesn't matter what men think of you."

She curled up beside me and pressed her chin into my shoulder. "It matters what this man thinks of me."

That's it. Everything she did in that moment worked together to activate a switch inside of me. To tackle my self-control and detonate a bomb that would destroy any chance of love. Not that I loved Miranda. I couldn't.

Well, I did love her. Not romantically. Not yet. I couldn't.

Could I?

All I knew is if our lips touched … the temptations would outnumber me. I'd fall into the trap and regret it. If I did love her, or could love her, it needed to be the right way. I will never forget the day Ella walked in on me and Sophie Monahan making out on the basement couch. I was seventeen. Ella was in eighth grade, I think. She smirked and with such certainty declared, "The door to a woman's heart is not her vagina."

From that day on I remembered her words every time my hands wandered a woman's body and I knew, without a doubt, that if I continued I'd soon enter the wrong door and end up with nothing more than another dent in my heart. Except for Ashleigh. I left her with more than a dent. A blow so hard my heart barely functioned anymore. And if it did, I didn't know it.

Miranda deserved better.

She fell asleep against me. Her chest expanding and hitting my arm. Eventually, after torturing myself with dreams of kissing her, I fell asleep too.

THE SLIGHTEST HINT OF DAYBREAK AND I COULD NO LONGER sleep. So I watched Miranda until she woke up and without much time to think, she supported her head on her hand and said, "Do you believe in God?"

I shrugged. "Good morning to you too."

"Oh, good morning. So do you?"

I put both hands behind my head. "Do you always wake up with profound questions on your mind?"

"It's not profound. Just like asking if you believe in aliens or not. Yes or no?"

"It's more complicated for me."

"How? You either believe God exists or you don't? Evolution? Big Bang? What do you believe?"

"Why do I get the feeling I'm being attacked before I've had a chance to open my eyes?"

She sat up, crossed one leg over the other, and leaned back. "I'm serious, Derek. I want to know."

I sighed, then gulped. I didn't know. Truth is, I didn't want to know. If God existed then I'd go straight to hell anyway, so I preferred ignoring the question altogether.

"Well," she said. "I believe in him and I realized on this little vacation that I miss him. The storm made me think of him."

"How do you miss an invisible person?"

"Clearly you don't know God."

I sat up too. "Clearly. So there's your answer. If I don't know him, how can I believe in him?"

"Exactly." She pat my shoulder. "You need to get to know him."

"And how do you get to know invisible things?"

"First, you realize he's not invisible and go on a quest to discover how he makes himself visible."

I rubbed my temples. "I'm not a stupid guy. At least I don't think I am, but it's debatable. This is too much for me to think about though. I'd much rather talk about the weather."

She unzipped the tent and stepped out. "Weather is nice. Damp ground. Sunny sky. From what I can see."

I stepped out and she wrapped her hand around my forearm. Couldn't help but notice the increase in her touches.

"You know," she said. "You helped me get rid of a ton of stuff from my bag of burdens. I'm thankful for you, but I wish you'd release yours. Whatever you're hiding. I can see it."

"I'm hiding a past that's darker and worse than anything you can imagine, and if your God is real he definitely hates me."

"Doubt it."

"I don't."

She let me have the last word. Thankfully. I made her breakfast as she watched me. Never took her eyes off. I felt like a piece of art hanging crooked on a wall. The kind people stare at for hours trying to make up abstract meanings for every stroke when really the guy just slapped some paint on a canvas to pay his rent.

"They say every cynical person is really just a discouraged idealist," I said.

Miranda laughed. "Who told you that?"

"Ella told me once. In case you haven't noticed she tends to be a little on the idealistic side. I always told her she hoped for things that would leave her hopeless. She insisted that I was idealistic too, except she said I gave up easily and turned my unfulfilled dreams into cynicism."

"And you believed her or no?" She held up her hand. "Wait. I'm gonna guess no."

"I'm a skeptical optimist."

She smiled. "Or a hopeful pessimist?"

Chapter Eleven
Miranda

After breakfast under the magical wisteria heaven, I took my journal and went for a short walk alone. Derek hiked somewhere too. In the opposite direction. I asked him to stay close in case I got scared. He laughed, but I trusted him.

I had so many guy friends throughout life that my closeness with Derek didn't strike me as odd, but I was starting to feel like the platonic level had somehow vanished. Or perhaps never existed at all. When we looked at each other something was different. And I found myself wanting to say, "I love you," during various moments, but I refrained. Not even sure I knew what love was.

It's a fine word.

Love.

A word I tossed around many times before. A word I never tried to understand before tainting it with guys who didn't know how to live from their heart.

Derek scared me. Not because he was a bad guy. Or a mean person. He scared me because he had tucked his heart so far inside of him that I feared I would fall in love with him and he wouldn't be able to return the favor. I know because I did it to so many other guys. I'll never forget the night I broke up with Mark over the phone. He showed up at my door in tears. Kind of annoyed, I tried to get him to leave, but he insisted we talk about everything. So we sat in his car and he made me tell him why I thought it wouldn't work between us. I gave him a few reasons and he rebutted them all with things like, "I can change. People change." I finally walked away that night and felt horrible. Honestly. I didn't like breaking hearts, but I guess that's part of my own selfishness. My preference to protect myself at the cost of others. I stayed single for a while after Mark. Didn't want to hurt anyone else and only dated people who obviously didn't want anything serious. Somehow I managed to keep my wall up and prevent love from seeping through the cracks.   I didn't blame him Derek. I understood. Whatever happened in his past had left its fangs in his flesh.

But I wanted to know him.

I sat down against a tree by the lapping water and pressed my pen into the blank page. The only way I knew how to process my feelings was by story. So I began.

June 11

The Adventures of Turtle and Lizzy

Never in a million years did Lizzy ever think she'd find a creature as intriguing as Turtle. He often retreated into his shell out of fear. Not sure what he feared, but Lizzy found herself sitting by him and waiting for him to embrace the world around him.

It seemed, however, that Lizzy spent most of her time stroking his back and waiting for something that would never happen. Had she not done that so many times before with various other creatures, perhaps she would have experienced a wee more hope.

Turtle helped Lizzy. Now Lizzy wanted to help Turtle. Not because she felt bad and wanted to repay him. Not at all. She just wanted Turtle to be happy. Maybe she had already fallen in love with him. Crazy how love can sneak up on you when you're not paying attention. Like a basketball left on a staircase. Step on it when your joyfully skipping down the steps and you fall. Head first. And love catches you. Like a safety net you never knew existed.

That's something Lizzy enjoyed. Most creatures took baby steps down the canyon, across the canyon, and back up the canyon. Even the birds feared their wings and walked with the other animals. Not Lizzy. She

took one look at the other side and knew she'd rather die leaping than spend her life walking to the other side and possibly never make it.
So when Turtle stood at the edge of the cliff, peering over and wondering how a reptile could make it to the other side without falling thousands of feet to its death, Lizzy pat his back and said, "Faith is hoping for things you can't see. If you believe, anything is possible."

But Turtle didn't understand. Didn't want to understand. Lizzy didn't expect him to. Not yet. Sometimes you have to completely lose faith in yourself in order to trust something else, and he obviously believed in himself more than the wind that would carry him safely to the other side.

Perhaps, Lizzy thought, if she jumped first maybe Turtle would follow. So, she did.

But he didn't follow.

I DIDN'T REMEMBER FALLING ASLEEP, SO WHEN I WOKE UP alone on the rocky shore I jumped up and looked around. Completely forgot where I was. After collecting my thoughts and calming down, I noticed Derek tossing rocks into the water a few yards away. He hadn't left me alone. With the spiders. And snakes.

Very kind of him. Very kind indeed.

I opened my journal back up and the scratchy handwriting after mine confused me for a second, until I realized Derek must've read my entry and added more himself. I looked at him, but he pretended not to notice me. How embarrassing that he read my journal. I'm normally an open book, but only when I choose to be.

I focused on his handwriting and read.

Lizzy thinks she's jumped to the other side of the canyon but it's an optical illusion…. She feels like she has rid her past and ripped every arrow from her heart, but that doesn't happen in two days on a camping trip….. They say it takes twice as long to heal a wound as it did to make

65

it…. Not sure how true that is, but either way Lizzy and Turtle both have a choice to make every day…. To try to be better, happier, nice and kind, and possibly find a way to love, or to dwell in the pain and live in an emotional prison…. Yeah, so, Lizzy seems to be making the right steps toward a happy, better person.

Where does that leave ole Turtle? Old. That's where. Old and tortured by nightmares that are so vivid he can barely sleep 5 hours a night without wanting to die….. and Turtle doesn't fabricate, if anything he withholds.

But I guess there's one good thing. He found a lizard who is really sweet and pretty and she sometimes wonders if she loves him. He sometimes wonders the same.

And although it may not be reality, the wondering makes him want to live again.

Well, certainly an array of grammatical errors. Ever heard of a period? You know, the thing that ends a sentence. Writing is not his speciality, but that's okay. *Stop ignoring his words*, the one side of myself said to the other side of myself. *I need to ignore those words*, the other side said to the one side. *You are falling in love with him and you like it.* Not sure which side of me said that to which side, but I ignored her. Or me.

I shook my head. Am I the only person who has conversations with various sides of myself? Internal wars on the field of my heart. My heart is a battlefield. Cue the eighties dance moves. Yes. Okay.

Right.

Derek finally walked toward me. I stood and followed him back up the hill, in silence, ignoring him trying to ignore me. And the growing, swelter-ing, give-me-a-fan-so-I-can-calm-down tension between us.

Growing up my brothers always told me I wanted things I couldn't have or things I wanted to fix. And once I got the prize or realized the person wasn't fixable, I left, looking for a new challenge or project. As much as I hate to admit, perhaps everyone had been more right about me than my very self. Derek was a challenge. And a project, at least it seemed so. Yet, I didn't find myself drawn to him in the same way. I didn't feel like a heroine. He didn't feel like a hero. We felt like . . . Turtle and Lizzy. Two lost souls swimming in a fish bowl.

I hummed the melody and waited for Derek to recognize it. When he didn't say anything I asked him to name the tune.

"Not sure," he said, out of breath as he pulled the wisteria vines and walked through the entrance.

"You don't know Pink Floyd?" I said.

"I've heard them."

"Not a fan?"

"I'm more of a Charles Mingus kinda guy."

"Who's that?"

He grabbed his bag and handed me crackers and cheese.

I took a handful and said, "So, can you tell me what happened in your past that's so bad?"

He closed his eyes, then looked past me, reflecting. "You're the only person I've wanted to spill my heart to."

I smiled inside. Maybe my face did too.

"Come with me," he said. "I want to show you something."

We walked through thorn bushes, over fallen branches, and under the beams of sunlight sword fighting in the trees.

Something bit my foot. I looked down and screamed. Derek poked a stick into the grass and laughed at me.

"Something just bit me." I held my ankle as it tingled with pain. "I think I'm poisoned."

"You're not poisoned." He laughed again.

"My entire foot is in pain. Like all hot and tingly." I winced. "We have to go. Now."

He held my shoulder. "It's burn hazel, Lizzy. Just a plant. When you touch it your skin feels burned."

I knelt and looked at my foot. "It really hurts."

"Let's walk a few steps further. We're almost there and I know of something that may help."

"Thanks, Turtle."

A few seconds later we walked into a clearing. No trees. Only grass the color of Granny Smith apples standing between us and a cliff. Or maybe an embankment. I couldn't tell.

"Thought you were afraid of heights?" I elbowed him as we walked.

He nudged me back. "It's not as high as it looks."

We stood at the edge and peered over. Thousands and thousands, and I mean thousands, of wild flowers. Mostly red from what I could tell. Flecks of deep burgundy amidst a sea of green, floating in the breeze like little boats captured by the golden lines of the sun. I gasped. Derek stood, hands in his pockets, back straight, shoulders high, and grinned. Like a boy on his papa's lap. I looked around, then back to him.

His eyes locked with mine and my heart rate picked up. I turned and stood in front of him, the red boats behind me. His deep, mysterious, slightly squinted eyes in front of me. He took my hands and shifted his weight to his left leg. The sunset warmed his brown hair, creating auburn highlights even in his newly grown facial hair. My eyes stumbled over his lips, down his neck, chest, then to his hands, tightly locked with mine.

My pulse, hasty with passion, surged through my veins. There. That feeling again. The one where I can no longer feel my legs and every part of me wants to fall into him. Melt into him. Be part of him.

He ran his hands up my arms, to my shoulders, and stopped at my neck. My knees. They couldn't bear it. I closed my eyes and gently held his arms as he moved a hand up my neck. I could no longer feel the burns from that plant. Tingly pricks of passion took over. His thumb stopped by my temple and his palm rested below my ear, cradling my head with a fragile strength. I opened my eyes and swept his gaze into me.

He leaned toward me, then hesitated. Unsure of what a kiss would do to our budding friendship, just like me. Would it blossom or destroy it altogether? Neither of us wanted a broken heart.

I waited.

He waited.

The wildflower meadow behind me waited. Anticipating. Where would the story of my life go next?

He moved his thumb across my cheek and traced my brow, then

somehow, without me realizing it, his lips tangled with mine. My eyes closed and our chins touched, but I saw images of him smiling as we kissed. He pulled his lips away. Too early. And pressed his forehead into mine. I waited a minute. Caught my breath. Then kissed him again. My legs weakened even more and I lost my balance. His hand gripped my arm as I fell backwards and rolled down the hill. My back whacked against something and my leg twisted and seared with pain. I landed in the field of red petals and scrunched my face.

Out of nowhere, he knelt beside me. "You okay?"

"My back and left leg hurt."

"How bad?"

I shrugged. "You look good in flowers."

"Can you move your toes?"

I tried.

"Did you try?"

"Yes."

He lifted me into his arms and carried me through the meadow.

"Wait," I said. "Can you hand me a flower or two? Or just bend down a little and I can get it."

He bent his legs so I could pick one. And I picked three. I wanted to save them. Just in case. You never know what kind of moments you may want to remember forever. I didn't know, but just in case....

Chapter Twelve
Derek

There are two kinds of beautiful. There's the kind that makes you turn your head and look with your eyes. Then, there's the rare beauty that blinds you. That's the kind that sticks with you forever. The kind that steals your vision and when you finally open your eyes you see the world differently. More vivid and colorful and beautiful.

Like her.

She affected me. Infected me, rather.

As I carried her to the tent, wrapped her leg in a make-shift splint, and brushed the hair from her face, I knew she had infected me with some kind of desire. A desire I couldn't yet place. All I knew was the day before I questioned life and now I simply enjoyed it. No questions. No opinions. Isn't that strange? Derek Rhodes? Speechless?

My sister would be happy. Perhaps my mother too.

I packed our stuff, carried her down the hill as the sun finally caved in and offered us the moon, and went back up to fetch the bags. By the time I came down she had decided to wait until morning to go to the hospital.

"You sure?" I said. "I have an extra boat docked here. It's only a few yards around that bend. It's actually my friend Aaron's, but he said I could use it."

"Thought you said no one else has ever been here?"

"He hasn't."

She crossed her arms over her chest and leaned back into the large rocks behind her. Her eyes searched mine. "Why'd you bring me here?"

"I used to be like you. I sought attention in several ways and eventually rebelled against it all, but it seriously backfired in my face."

She motioned for me to continue.

"Oh, what the hell. I'm attracted to you. Whether I want to be or not, since the first time I saw you at my sisters wedding. Those little pink flowers stuck in your violet hair. Your pink dress and green scarf that you named Willow Tree. The way you walked. The way you laughed. The way you so willingly left their house with a strange guy you had never met before. Not to mention the talk we had while parked behind the grocery store. You were intelligent and you fascinated me. You were more than a body. You were a mind and a heart. I liked that, I guess." I shook my head. "I'm sorry. I said too much."

"I don't know what to say…" she said. "So wait, I still don't get why you brought me here. And why did you want to get rid of my luggage?"

"I wanted you to see that you don't need all that to be beautiful. Or loved. Or whatever. Your identity isn't wrapped up in your hobbies, hair colors, or clothes. I wanted you to be free of that and see how beautiful you are like this."

"Like what?"

"At rest."

She uncrossed her arms and clasped her hands, then peered at me though strands of unwashed hair. "This scares me, Derek."

"What?"

"This feeling I have when I look at you."

I sat down beside her. Took her hand and traced her palm. Truth is, I was nervous too. Worried that we'd go back home and forget this experience happened. She'd lose those flowers she picked and our first kiss would be the last. Two broken hearts are difficult to mold into one. Too many pieces to find first. She deserved someone better. Someone whole. Someone who could make her whole.

I held her under the moon's sheepish grin as peaceful waves glided to shore, rocking us both to sleep. I woke up every hour or so, counted stars, then fell back asleep. Repeated until the sun broke through the clouds and glistened on the waves and her eyelids. I kissed them. And she woke too.

"I'm gonna take you to the hospital now," I said. "Then, I'll take you home. After that, we'll pretend this never happened."

She kissed me. Soft and quick. Then, without a single word spoken between us, we took the boat back to my car, loaded it up, and drove to the nearest hospital. I didn't tell her why I couldn't go inside, but she didn't mind. She braved it alone and texted me when she was done. I picked her up, helped her into the car, and drove back to Pennsylvania.

As we passed through Maryland she started texting a mile a minute.

"Who's that?" I said.

"Heidi. Her little one is recovering well from surgery. Patrick and her set a date for their wedding. She said they're going to have it at the skate park."

"That will be . . . different."

She smiled. "And what's your ideal wedding?"

"It'll never happen."

"You don't think you'll ever get married?"

"If I do, the last thing I'll be worried about is where it is and what she wears."

We barely talked the rest of the drive. She slept on and off. I was amazed at how well she handled the pain. She refused the pain killers and took some extra arnica I had in my car. I doubt it helped much in her situation, but she seemed strong. Must've been the tomboy from days gone by. Her fracture wasn't too bad, but still. It hurts. Course I had never broken a bone, at least not my own, so I guess I didn't know for sure.

We finally parked in front of her apartment building. Awkward silence. I didn't know whether to get out or stay still. She pulled her old journal out of her bag and handed it to me. "I want you to have this."

I didn't ask why or what I was supposed to do with it. Couldn't even muster the words, "Thank you." Wasn't sure if I should've been thankful anyway. Why would she give me her journal?

"You are one of the few people who truly knows me." She kissed my cheek. "Let's promise to never let a relationship ruin our friendship."

I didn't respond. Not sure I wanted to promise such a thing. Obviously I wasn't sure of much.

I wanted to carry her up the steps, but she insisted she'd be okay with her hot pink cast and wooden crutches. So I watched as she limped away and turned to blow me a kiss just before slipping into the doorway.

I missed her already. Almost felt unnatural to say goodbye to her and I didn't know what to make of that feeling. A feeling I'd never felt before with a woman. Things were so different with Ashleigh. So much darker, lust-driven, and bitter. A memory I wished I didn't have. I pulled into the streets of Philadelphia. One red light after another and I made my way to the highway that would take me back home. Two states away from my best friend.

Without a doubt, that drive home was the longest drive of my life. Loneliest too.

Chapter Thirteen
Miranda

A few days after my trip with Derek, I settled down for bed when a text from a strange number appeared on my phone. Didn't recognize the area code. A simple, *Hey, Miranda. Is it still your number?* I asked who it was and quickly received his response. I couldn't believe it. After all these years, he came back. I thought about him so often, wondering if we'd reunite and hit it off. Wondering if he'd be the one I'd give my heart to.

Me: *Oliver?? From the beach??*

Oliver: *Yes. It's me. Look, I'm really sorry I never called.*

Me: *I didn't think you actually would. Why are you now?*

Oliver: *I know we had a typical beach fling, and most people never talk again. I haven't been able to stop thinkin about you since. I know it's been years. I just found your number when I was packing up to move. Can we meet up?*

Me: *I'm not interested in flings.*

Oliver: *Me neither.*

Me: *Then what?*

Oliver: *I want to see you.*

Me: *We barely know each other. It was one night. One kiss.*

Oliver: *Can we meet and see?*

Miranda: *It's late. I will text you tomorrow. Are you visiting from the UK?*

Oliver: *I'm here in the States for good now.*

Only me. Only in my life would the guy I dreamt about for years come back and want to see me. Exactly like I always imagined and hoped. At exactly the wrong time. I didn't wash my shirt for weeks when I came home from the beach that year. Smelled his Tommy Hill cologne as I slept for days on end.

Oliver?

Really?

Oh dear. I propped my hot pink leg up on my bed and called Heidi. The only person I could trust with the details of my heart.

She answered. We got by on small talk for a few minutes, then I unveiled my heart. "Derek took me to this amazing place. Like a surreal escape from the world. Something I've only dreamed of seeing. Here's the thing, though. I think I started to fall in love with him."

"And that's bad?" she said. "You guys have been destined to fall in love since you first met. What's taking so long for you to realize that?"

"I can't, Heidi." I took a deep breath and surprised myself when a tear fought it's way to my cheek. "He's so closed off. Something's not right. And we're such great friends. He's my best friend, really. I've never been so close to another person. Every person I've dated falls out of love with me or realizes he never loved me in the first place. I'm so scared he will do the same and I can't bear the thought of not having him in my life at all."

"I don't think you can compare Derek to your exes."

"I'm not so sure."

"He's so much more mature."

"He is, but I don't know. I don't trust him in that way."

"Do you trust anyone?"

I didn't know how to answer that. I trusted myself. My ability to protect my heart from real pain by giving it to guys who I didn't like all that much to begin with. No strings attached.

"Well?" she said.

"I like falling in love without the pressure of commitment. I get to experience the fun beginning stage over and over without the blood, sweat, and tears."

"You realize how horrible that sounds, right?"

Not sure I did.

"Miranda, I'm saying this because I love you, but that is insanely selfish of you. To spend your life giving guys the wrong impression just so you can feel fuzzy sensations and not get your heart broken if they cheat on you. Do you really want to end up single in your forties, still going from man to man, all because you fear arguments and conflicts?"

I tried to swallow her words, but they got stuck in my teeth. "I don't fear conflict."

"Yes, you do. You fear that you'll actually give your heart to someone and he'll give it back when things get tough." Riley babbled in the background. "Patrick and I rarely argue, but when we do it's short-lived. When you love someone you want to work it out. Whatever it takes."

"I'm not good at conflict."

"Yeah. You run away and hide behind closed doors, then sweep it under the rug."

"You make me sound so desirable."

"We all have our cobwebs."

"There's this other guy though. I met him when I was at the beach for senior week years ago. I know, I know, but it was actually really sweet. We stayed up all night talking in the lifeguard chair and kissed as the sun rose. He's even British. You know how I love a nice accent."

"Don't get all Ella on me."

I laughed. "Anyway, he contacted me. Wants to meet."

"Suit yourself."

"What's that supposed to mean?"

"It means sometimes you have to sit back and let the people you love make mistakes."

"Well, thanks."

"Derek is a good guy. You'll regret losing him."

"I'm never going to lose him. He's my friend. You can't break up with a friend."

I hung up with her and tried to convince myself. Derek didn't want a girlfriend anyway. We kissed, yes. We had good conversations, yes. I think I even enjoyed myself, but that didn't change the fact that Derek was a turtle hiding in an unbreakable shell. I didn't trust guys like that. Whatever he kept hidden I honestly didn't know if I could bear hearing it. It seemed bad. As a friend, I could handle it. Help him. Love him and be a shoulder to cry on. As a girlfriend? I didn't know. That was the biggest problem.

Not knowing.

My phone beeped again. Another text.

Derek: *Liz, did you get the envelope I put in your bag?*

Me: *What envelope?*

Derek: *Look for it.*

Me: *Oh, found it here. Opened it just now. You didn't have to do that.*

Derek: *Go buy yourself some new clothes whenever you stop limping around.*

Me: *Well, I guess I'll accept since you threw out most of my stuff, but only this once. I still haven't asked how you have stashes of money to throw away.*

Derek: *I never throw it away.*

Me: *Ok. Fair enough. Thanks for the trip. I learned a lot and I really appreciate it.*

Derek: *Glad to hear it.*

Me: *A guy from my past texted me today. He wants to get together. Should I?*

The glowing screen didn't beep. I waited for the little dots to show up on my iPhone, saying he was responding, but they didn't show up. I started to type, erased, started again, erased, then finally settled with a simple text.

Me: *You don't even want to get married, Derek.*

Derek: *I don't, but if I did it would be with you.*

Me: *I can't marry someone who hides his past. I've spent my entire life being a savior to guys like that. I don't have the energy anymore.*

Derek: *I'm not looking for a savior.*

Me: *This won't work. It just can't work. Let's stay friends, okay? You date other people, if you ever want to. And I will. That way we can always be friends and never say goodbye forever.*

Derek: *I will never say goodbye forever. Not to you. I'm sorry. I don't know what's gotten into me. This isn't like me. I don't even know if I've ever felt this way before. I'm sorry. I won't bring it up again.*

Me: *You've never felt what way before?*

Derek: *Never mind. Goodnight, Lizzy. Good luck with your guy.*

Something about our conversation irritated me, but then again that was typical of us. Another reason I couldn't bring myself to be with him. What if we spent our entire lives bickering? What if we started our first night as husband and wife by arguing about what kind of wine to drink? I needed someone more like me. Someone full of spunk and energy. Someone who drank deep from the well of life and relished every moment, every experience, as though it may be the last. Derek taught me a lot. I was thankful for him. And for the first time in a long time I felt relieved of the heavy burden

I carried so long. But I couldn't make him happy. Not until he found happiness alone first.

I rubbed my head and turned off my phone. The darkness reminded me of him. Our last night on that island. He held me the entire night. Woke me up with gentle kisses on my eyelids. I couldn't love him, though. What if he ended up like my father? Like a creaky old room in an abandoned house, void of character and hauntingly stoic, hidden....

I shook the thoughts away, watched them drift into the darkness and out of sight, then closed my eyes and imagined Oliver kissing me on the lifeguard chair as the Atlantic ocean shined with the sun's early morning pinks and purples.

The last thought I remember before falling asleep stuck with me until I woke up. I don't like who I am.

I just didn't know who else to be.

TIME FOR A CHANGE. I LIMPED MY WAY TO MY FAVORITE SALON and requested rich, chocolatey brunette. No more funky colors. I wanted to appear normal for Oliver.

As Gabbie, the young girl with perfect blonde curls, made me look new again I thought of Derek. I felt bad for him. I really did. But how could I be with someone who didn't want to be with anyone?

"You look deep in thought," Gabbie said as she unfolded the foil on my head. "Everything okay?"

"Guy problems."

"I understand." She placed a few pieces of foil in a bowl beside her. "My boyfriend of ten years just broke up with me. I don't even know how to be myself without him."

"Ten years? What happened?"

"We met junior year of high school. Been together since. I've been pushing for an engagement ring and I think I pushed too far." She led me to the shampoo chair and tilted my head back. "It's like I started to value the ring more than him. He felt that."

"Ten years though?" I closed my eyes as she massaged my head and rinsed the dye. "That's a long time. Why wouldn't he marry you?"

"Afraid. Of a lot of things." She wrapped my hair into a towel and took me back to the mirror and chair. "He didn't think he could provide. Didn't think he could give me what I wanted."

"What did you want?"

"A family."

"He doesn't want kids?"

"No. So, what about your situation?"

"Well, I'm torn. There's this guy. I'm really good friends with him. He is so interesting. Smart. Mysterious. Gorgeous. Need I say more?" I laughed. "But I don't know. Maybe I'm like your boyfriend. I am so afraid of being rejected or cheated on or left in the dust for a career or car or video games."

She blow-dried my hair as we both thought about my words and our own love lives. Maybe it seemed complicated to others, but to me it was simple. Don't let anyone in and you won't get hurt. Let them in and you welcome the opportunity to get hurt. I wanted marriage and a pregnant belly. I wanted life with a partner. A best friend. A lover. Someone to experience ups and downs and in-betweens. Like any other normal girl in the world I dreamed of my wedding day, but what if the big bad wolf dressed like Prince Charming and ate my head off?

Clearly, I had trust issues.

I made a pact with myself. Go and see Oliver after good ole doc removed my cast, and have fun one last time. No strings attached. If I fell for him, I wouldn't prevent it. And if I didn't, I'd force Derek to tell me what he kept inside.

She finished my hair and spun the chair around. I analyzed myself. Dark curly hair down to my elbows. No highlights. Had been a long time since my reflection looked so normal.

"What do you think?" Gabbie said.

"Not sure what to think." I tilted my head. "You did a great job. It's just been a while since I've had something so close to my natural color."

"You look so beautiful. Kind of like a modern Audrey Hepburn."

I smiled. "Well, thank you, Gabbie. Wonderful as always." I hugged her. As I did to mostly everyone I met. "Let me know how it goes with that precious heart of yours."

I walked to my car, imagining Gabbie going to see a movie with friends.

In walks a super attractive guy. Sits down right next to her. Their elbows touch. A few butterflies and glances later, they smile at each other. By the end of the movie they've spoken enough with their eyes. They exchange numbers and enjoy each other for years to come.

People became stories to me. Happy stories with happy endings. Matt always considered me an optimist on pixie sticks. One too many doses of sugar. If only he read my journal. He'd see that I painted life around me beautiful. And I hoped things ended up the way I drew them. When it came to my own life, however, I painted it as I saw it. No bells. No whistles. Just me.

Beyond the bottles of hair dye and conversations with strangers ... I was a girl. A girl no one knew. And the only one who cared enough to try to get to know me was the man who wouldn't let me in.

Chapter Fourteen
Derek

I read most of Miranda's journal. Stared at the pages for a while after I finished. Found it interesting that her handwriting changed. Seemed to depend on her mood. Soft, bubbly letters for content entries. All capitals and slanted toward the right for excited entries. An ancient italicized cursive for obviously fabricated lives of people around her. And the sad entries were quick, messy strokes of barely legible words. Often too far over and under the lines. She signed every entry with a single *M*.

A lot to digest. Like a starving child given a feast after eating bug-sprinkled rice for five years. Partly wanting to push the plate away and the other part wanting to turn into a gluttonous fool. I didn't know which to be, so I analyzed her handwritings and ignored the words. Until I forced myself to go back and read the one entry I couldn't stop thinking about. I did the math. She would've just turned nineteen.

To myself, the only one who really listens,

Happy birthday to me. My dad's cutting words never bothered me before. Not sure why they did tonight. Also not sure why I reacted the way I did, but I regret it now. The bloody lip wasn't worth it. Neither was the pain on my mother's face. Neither was the pain on my face.

I'm tired. It's 2:53am and I worked a ten hour shift today, plus four hours of school. Community College, honestly, what is this? It's high school tied up with a more expensive bow. And I had to pay for it all myself.

I've decided from this day on to never give my heart to a man. Not unless he fights like crazy to get it. And I mean, really fights. None of this waking sleeping beauty with a kiss nonsense or sending people around the world with a glass slipper. Why do girls find that stuff so romantic anyway? No. It's kind of dumb. The prince never really does anything. He's just a prince and because of that the poor, poor girl is supposed to fall madly in love with him and await his rescue.

That's not me. After all this with my dad I'm pretty much scared of ever putting a ring on my finger and ending up like my mom, no matter how well the shoe fits.

If a man ever comes along he better fight like William Wallace for this princess. All the way to his death if necessary. Because that is the true cost of love, isn't it?

Killing the self to make room for others.

Not saying I wouldn't fight too. I would. I'd die for the right man. In a heartbeat. Give everything I am for him. All I want is someone who will do the same.

Why don't guys like that exist anymore? Or if they do... Why don't I meet them? They all break up with me. Even the ones I never found attractive. I'm never good enough for them. Never worth fighting for. And the ones who are all about me are the ones I can't stand to be around for more than five minutes.

Enough of the pity party, Self. Time to go to bed and wake up to a new start. I don't need a man to be happy. I don't need a woman either. Friends and lovers come and go. The only person I can rely on is you, Self. I feel bad for what I said to my dad tonight. He's the coldest person I've ever known. But he didn't deserve what I said. I guess I still have some dying to do as well.

Nice talking to ya, my dear self. Thanks for listening.

Hopefully I can sleep now.

Love,
-M-

Miranda played the strong card well. Maybe that's why she gave me these yellowed pages. Maybe she wanted someone to see that she was weaker than she seemed. She didn't want a man to sweep her off her feet and carry her away. She wanted someone to hold her hand and live an adventure with her. No carrying involved. Only leaning on each other when necessary.

I thought she used guys. One of the many girls who flirt for attention and spend hours making themselves pretty to count how many heads they can turn. I'm not dumb. It's obvious when a woman is using a man for validation of her beauty. Which is why I looked down in public. Counted the tiles and blocks of cement, analyzed my shoe strings, anything to be mistaken for another check mark in the "How Pretty Am I?" contest. That sounds bad, but my ex changed the way I saw women.

My sister is beautiful. And the thing about her is she doesn't flaunt it. That's what I grew up around. When Ashleigh walked into my life that abnormally warm fall night, I was hypnotized. Perfect body, always pristine, arrogance I naively misplaced as confidence, and she wanted me. I tried to get her away. Many times. Just wasn't the kind of girl you take home to the folks. But she insisted. I was the check mark she needed to have, not because I'm the next Leonardo DiCaprio, simply because I wasn't an easy check mark to get. When I finally caved, I ended up in bed, alone, wondering why I couldn't calm my heart rate.

Eventually switched my degree for her and followed her all the way to a masters degree. Spent my twenties buying her fake nails and designer clothing. She never loved me. She never loved much. And she took me to hell with her.

That's what women had become to me. Attention grapplers. Some call it insecurity. Others call it arrogance. I call them both pride. The inability to find contentment in who you really are and instead focusing your entire life on what you wish you could be. Simply for some kind of false and transitory pleasure.

That's the reason I took Miranda away to my nook in the world. I didn't want to see her end up like Ashleigh. Or me. No one deserves to live such an empty depressing life. Especially not Miranda.

I tried to call her. No answer. A few minutes later she called back.

"Hey," she said. "I'm buying some clothes right now actually. Thank you for that. And you'll be happy to know I've dyed my hair back to brown. A normal color."

"Is that right?" I laughed. "And how does it feel?"

"Normal is weird to me, but I'm getting used to it. Don't get too excited though. I still love the funky colors."

"I don't want to change you, Liz. Just wanted you to realize you don't need to change to be happy or beautiful. Rest. That's all."

"If you say so." Something clanked and banged. "Sorry. Dropped the phone. I get my cast off soon. Can't wait. Hey, did you find another job yet?"

"No."

"Are you looking?"

"Not in a hurry. I have more money than I know what to do with."

"You still won't tell me why?"

"No."

"I have a date next weekend."

"Yeah. Is he everything you dreamed of? Golden hair and great big biceps?"

"Um." She laughed. "Did you just describe Stretch Armstrong?"

"I want you to be happy, Lizzy." I set her journal on my bed. "Read your diary today."

No response.

"It was interesting."

"You're the only person in the world who's read that, you know."

"That's what friends are for." I picked it back up. "I want you to know that you deserve someone who will fight for you. Whatever that means. You are worth it and I hope you find someone. I'm sorry I can't be that. I don't know how to live, much less die."

"What happened to you, Derek? Tell me, please."

I breathed heavy. Waited. Not easy to speak of the things I'd locked away. I almost believed they'd happen all over again if I relived them in my memory. "It started when I was in college. Met a girl and fell into her trap. Super manipulative. Vindictive. Rude. Cocky. Don't remember what I fell for now that I think of it." I shook my head. "Anyway, I changed my major to follow her. Wasn't what I wanted to do. You know how you said in your journal that you have to kill yourself to make room for others? Well, I killed myself alright. Killed off every good part of me and made room for a whole lot of horrible stuff."

"What did you do?"

Every time I tried to speak the truth it never made it past my mind. My hands shook. The phone shook. My voice, if I were speaking, would had been shaking too. "I will write it down. Next time we see each other you can read it. It's too hard to say out loud, especially over the phone."

"Okay. Fair enough." She paused. We held the phone to our ears in silence for a few minutes. I heard her pay the cashier, walk out of the store, and shut her car door, but we still said nothing. We did that sometimes. Enjoyed knowing we were there without the need to speak. Eventually she broke the silence. "I want you to know that I will always, always be here for you. Okay? I will never tell your secrets to anyone and I will always be on your side."

"Thanks, Miranda." I smiled, wishing I could see her face. "Take a picture of yourself and text me. I'm gonna get a quick shower and maybe get some groceries."

We hung up. Her picture came through a few minutes later. I dropped the phone. Picked it back up. Stared for a few minutes. Then typed back, *You were beautiful with pink, purple, blue, and green hair, but right now you are stunning. Stunningly normal. :)*

I took a shower and read her text after I got dressed. *Yeah, yeah. Thanks, Turtle. Best buds forever.*

I needed to win her heart. And if that meant spilling my own all over the place, I guess that's what I needed to do.

Another text came through. *I wear my heart on a shoestring. And so do you.*

Me: *But you wear those converse shoes or some kind of heel. And neither of those have shoestrings.*

Miranda: *Exactly.*

Me: *Does that mean we keep our hearts far from reach?*

Miranda: *Yes.*

Me: *What about your date?*

Miranda: *I have been with many people. Too many. I enjoy that fun first kiss feeling. But I've kept my heart on a shoestring. Far from anyone's hands.*

Me: *Why waste your lips on people who won't admire them forever?*

Took her a while to respond. Something changed between us. Almost overnight. Before we spent more time bickering and annoying each other. Now we talked about love and life. We were opening up our chests and revealing the hidden parts. I enjoyed it. Even if it was just a text message conversation, but her delay made me question her enjoyment. She got quiet for a reason. Maybe she sensed my growing desire for her and couldn't receive it.

She finally responded. Only it was her number calling mine. "Sorry. Matt called. He said Max is missing."

"Missing?"

"He ran away." Her voice quivered. "Max is my autistic brother."

"I remember who he is. What happened?"

She didn't answer, but her sobs pinched my nerves. I couldn't stand hearing her cry.

"I'm coming right now," I said, then grabbed my keys and headed for my car. I put the phone on speaker and left it on my lap as I drove. She sniffed the entire time, but never said a word.

Neither did I.

A few hours later I parked. "I'm here." We hung up and I texted Ella, *I'm again to help Miranda look for Max. Can I stay with you guys this week? Really not interested in another few hours of driving and I want to be here until he's found.*

She responded. *Of course. I'm with Lydia and her wee one. Gavin and Matt are already looking.*

I locked my car and stood on the curb, wondering how I ended up here. At a girls apartment. With my heart on a shoestring suddenly on my sleeve. Almost, at least.

I walked upstairs and knocked on her door. She opened, wiped her face on her sleeve, and fell into my arms. I scooted in the door, closed it, and held her for a few minutes. Her hair smelled like a garden. I put my chin on her head and inhaled. She curled her arms up between us, her palms on my chest, and spoke. "It's my fault."

"How is this your fault?"

She shook her head and pulled away. "Whenever my dad screamed at my mom he always brought up Max and how his life was so much better before he came along. I was always the one to go into Max's room to make sure he didn't hear. If he did hear I'd sit on his bed and rub his back. When I chose friends and guys over him, he was never the same and when I moved out I don't even want to know what happened with my dad." She caught her breath. "My mom said they were arguing. The typical. And the next morning Max was nowhere to be found. I should've been there. I should've stayed."

"Miranda, he's not your child. You aren't to blame. What if you were married and had your own kids? You can't always protect Max."

She still had her cast on. Looking for Max would be interesting. Definitely no hikes in the woods with that thing.

"I think I know where he might be. It's a place no one will know. Just Max and me."

"Let's go then."

Chapter Fifteen
Miranda

We drove to the doctor's office and Derek parked, looked around, then shrugged. "Are you sure this is the right place?"

I nodded, smiled. "When my mom had to work my dad refused to bring Max to his speech pathology appointments. Said he couldn't afford to take off work either. So I'd take him. He loved the steps here, so we'd go up and down, up and down, about seven thousand times, and then sit at the bottom and eat lunch. I always packed his favorite things. He loved it."

We walked inside, our elbows touching as our empty hands swung into each other. I wanted to hold his hand, but I was never the type to reach for a boy's hand. Made me nervous. Plus I didn't know how to be around Derek. If my heart was capable of love, it would love him so much. Butterflies danced in my stomach at the thought. I calmed them down and led Derek to the stairwell, preparing my hopeful heart for my little brother's face. Only he wasn't there.

Derek spun in a circle. I went up the steps and back down, then saw the paper in the corner, dirt smudged into the crumpled lines. I picked it up, turned it over in my hands, and smoothed it out. Derek leaned over my shoulder, his chest against my back. Magazine letters, torn and taped, formed words on the paper. I read them, cried, and read them again. Derek squeezed my shoulder.

"My brother wrote this," I said. "And he's never said a word in his life. Never written one either. Till now."

"What's it mean?"

I looked out the window above us. Sunlight warmed my wet face. I glanced back down to the paper and read aloud. "She has my favorite pen too. I am searching, not lost." I pressed it flat against my heart and turned to Derek. "My brother can speak. It may just be on paper, but he has a voice."

"What's it mean though? Where is he?"

"I think he's looking for me."

"Where do we go?"

"Let's try all the places I would take him."

Derek drove to the next place as I called Matt. "Hey, I found a letter from Max. I think he's looking for me. Derek and I are going to the park right now. Can you guys check a few places if I send you a list?"

"Yeah, but what do you mean by a letter?"

"He tore out letters from magazines and wrote something out. I can't believe it. I know it's him because he mentioned his favorite pen. I took his pen by an accident when I moved. He must be looking for it." I ran my hand over his colorful words. "I'm going to stop by and tell mom after the park, if he's not there. Police still searching?"

"Yeah. In rivers and lakes. Make sure you get in touch with mom. She hasn't gotten out of bed since."

We hung up. Derek turned the car off in front of a small park. One slide, two swings. That's it. Max and I spent many summer afternoons on those swings. His laugh filling the sky as we swung higher and higher. We'd walk from our house. It had been years since I sat on those swings. I still couldn't forgive myself for spending so much time with boys and ignoring Max. Years and years. Wasted. Gone. Never to return.

Maybe this was my chance to make it better. Maybe even Max knew that. We got back in the car but Derek didn't turn it on. He stared out the front window, a blank expression hugging his face. Hands in my lap, I waited. I knew him well enough to know he needed a few minutes to think before speaking about something important. I wondered if he'd finally open up to me.

"Can I ask you something?" he said, still looking ahead.

"You don't have to ask."

He cleared his throat and leaned back into his seat, spread his legs, then brought his knees together again. "Your God. Why does he create evil?"

"He doesn't."

"But"—he waved his hands in front of us—"all of this. Your autistic brother. Your rotten dad. Kidnappings. Gun fights. Who creates it all?"

I pulled my left foot under my right thigh, leaned back as well, and noticed my reflection in the side mirror. "We create evil. I think God just allows it."

"What kind of God allows all of this?" He sighed. "Is this really someone you want to love?"

"People should choose good on their own, not because they're programmed to. And if they choose evil, so be it. God isn't Hitler. He doesn't force people to act a certain way. They can choose and I think it's good to let them. Don't you think the good we do is even more meaningful because we could've just as easily chosen to do something bad?"

"You don't think he made your brother autistic?"

"Honestly, I have my thoughts about the cause of autism and no, it's not God. Once again it's people. What we've done and continue to do to the world around us and in effect, ourselves."

He put the keys in the ignition, but didn't twist. "But why would he allow it if he loves people? Why even create them? Why not end it all and be done?"

"I don't have answers, Derek. All I know is he allows it and I have a feeling it's to make us better people. Think of your favorite stories or movies. There's always evil. There's always something for the good guy to overcome. Otherwise he's not a hero, right? If all we do is spend our lives being served pancakes and pleasure, what kind of hero will we be? I think it's a gift. We get to fight for stuff we love. Instead of getting it all on a silver platter."

"That still doesn't make sense to me." He finally turned the car on. "And if that's true, how come you spend so much of your life choosing fun and games over the things that matter?"

His words sliced into my chest and punctured my heart. I almost bent over in real pain, but I couldn't. Frozen, I watched the park disappear as Derek drove to my parents house. He knew me. And he wasn't afraid to challenge me. Not many people cared enough to argue with me. To challenge my choices. Still, I battled between feeling loved and hurt. Misunderstood.

Don't go there, I told myself. Not to the land of the misunderstood.

I perched my elbow on the door frame and let the wind tug my hair. "Thank you," I said. Eyes closed, hair covering my eyes, I imagined what life would be like if I didn't fear commitment and rejection. How much could I love if I allowed myself? Would I be a hero or a coward?

Derek tapped his steering wheel and parked the car. "Tell me, what if you are the one who creates the evil? The one who does horrible things the complete opposite of love? Then what?"

"Are you implying that I do that?"

"No. Not at all. Just wondering what happens to the villains."

"I guess it depends on whether they can say sorry or not. And really mean it."

"What if they do, but it haunts them every day after?"

I reached for his hand. It shook so bad I thought it might fall off his wrist. He looked down. Serious. Almost stoic. But I knew underneath of his mask he felt something. He probably felt more than me.

"Let's go in," he said, avoiding exactly what he knew I'd ask next. That's okay though. I let him. Sometimes it's better to wait. To hold your breath a few seconds longer. It's scary to die, but sometimes it can be even scarier to live.

He walked behind me. Up the tiny sidewalk lined by flowers and bushes. I knocked on the door. Waited. Clenched my teeth and tightened my jaw.

Dad answered. Opened the door and walked back to the TV. Not as bad as I imagined. Derek followed me to Max's room. "Wait here," I said, then walked to Mom's room.

The door creaked as I opened it. She sat on the edge of her bed. Arms crossed over her chest. Hair dangling in front of her face. I moved closer. "Mom." She shook her head. I sat beside her. "Mom, I think I may know where he is."

"It's my fault. All of this." Pain seeped from her words and landed softly on my heart. I could relate. "I wanted another baby. Your father didn't know I stopped taking the pill. He doesn't know to this day. Thinks I got pregnant while taking it." Her arms tightened around her body. "I didn't know. If I had known everything Max would go through I would have stayed on the pill."

"Max is here now. You can't stuff him back in the womb. Why would you want to anyway?" I put my arm around her and rested my head against her shoulder. "Why don't you come with us? Help us find him."

"Your father won't let me."

I huffed and stood. "I've had it. This is not right."

She didn't look up as I stormed out of the room and downstairs. Derek stepped to the top of the stairs as I reached the bottom. I stood between my father and the television, arms at my sides, hands tightened into fists, and calmly, carefully chose my words. "I believe there is good in most people, but not you. I hate you. I hate what you've become. What you've done to this family. To mom. To me. To Matt and Mike and Max. You're selfish, mean, and the worst excuse of a man I've ever seen."

He stood. A crystal clear strength glazed over his eyes. The anger of a weak man masked with strength. I raised my chin and stared into his eyes. The vein in his forehead throbbed in the shape of a V. Derek, quiet as a winter night, stepped into the room. I saw his shadow move behind my dad, who now gripped my neck with thick, calloused fingers.

"I brought you into this world," he said. "I have no problems taking you out."

"I'm not afraid of dying." I pushed the words past his hand on my throat. "I'm afraid of not living. And no, it's not just your sperm I thank for that. I thank God."

He squeezed my neck, cutting off oxygen and forcing me to gag. I didn't care. Stared him down as my face filled with warm blood. He lifted me and pressed me against the wall by my neck. "If you were a boy I'd kill you."

Derek grabbed his arm and yanked his hand from my neck. "I'm a boy. How about you kill me?"

Dad spit in Derek's face and rolled his hand into a fist. "Who the hell are you and who do you think you are?"

"Kill me." Derek stepped closer so there was only an inch between his chest and my dad's. "If it makes you feel good, go ahead and kill me."

Dad shoved Derek's chest with both palms, yanked me by the arm, and forced us to the door. "Come in the house again and I swear I will rip the flesh right off your faces."

I pulled myself from his grip and ran up the stairs. "Mom, you're coming. Let's go."

To my surprise, she listened. When we reached the front door Dad was nowhere in sight. Derek left too. Mom walked beside me, head low, shoulders hunched. I sat her down in the passengers seat and took my place in the back. Derek started the car and turned to me, smiled. Blood dripped from his left eye down to his jaw.

"Are you okay?" I said, reaching for his face.

"Are you?" he said.

"Yes."

"What made him like that?"

My mom shifted in her seat, raised her head. "Maxwell. He was always distant and quiet, but not like this. Not until Max."

"Has he hit you?" Derek said, pulling into the suburban street.

"Never," she said.

"Max?"

"No. Matthew stayed out later than curfew one night and Lenny waited for him with a brick. Knocked the poor boy out. Other than that, no physical threats."

"Except what he just did to Miranda."

Mom turned and looked at me, then back to Derek. "And your eye?"

Derek nodded. "It's not a big deal. Just a little concerned for Max. Is it really safe for you all to live there with him?"

"I can't leave Lenny," Mom said. "I could never."

And I could never understand why the heck not.

Chapter Sixteen
Derek

Miranda's mother never buckled her seatbelt. Something about it bothered me. I always made passengers buckle up, but I couldn't ask her. Not now. Not with her son missing and her husband straight out of Jackass Central. Excuse me. But who in their right mind holds his daughter by the neck and blames an autistic child for ruining his life? I'm not one to talk. I had my fair share of horrible deeds, but what the hell?

My head throbbed, but I didn't let the ladies know. Last thing I wanted was someone fussing over me. Miranda seemed hopeful. Believed we'd find Max and bring him home safe. Or as safe as that home could be. Me? Not as optimistic, but is that a surprise? An autistic teenager roaming Philadelphia didn't sound promising, no matter how big the reward.

Miranda directed me to the next place, my mind hanging on to the sweetness of her voice. Something about all this made me feel closer to her. I wanted to explain everything. Be free of David Bennett and possibly win her heart. But how? When? No time ever seemed right.

I parked and opened my car door. Mrs. Ryan stayed in the car with no apparent intentions of moving. Miranda stepped out and linked her arm with mine, then wiped the blood from my face. Her eyes killed me. In a good way. Sent me to a place I longed to visit. A place I had yet to understand. All I knew is that place was the closest thing to paradise I'd ever seen. And I wanted it. Bad.

We walked down a path alongside a creek and about ten minutes later stood on a covered bridge. Old. The kind of thing that rattles when cars pass through. A perfect location for photography.

"What's that?" Miranda said. I saw nothing except a squirrel, trees, and a muddied creek. She jogged to a tree and knelt down. "It's gotta be Max. This is one of the magazines I gave him." She flipped through the glossy pages. "And it has missing letters."

We scanned the area for a note. A sign. A teenage boy. Nothing. My pessimism kicked up a few notches. Her optimism almost burst her heart like a balloon in the hands of a toddler.

Smiling, she rubbed the missing letters in the magazine as we walked back to the car. Mrs. Ryan didn't look up. Not once. Her mind and heart far from Philly. Reminded me of myself. The self I didn't want to be.

WE PARKED A BLOCK AWAY FROM AN ICE CREAM SHOP IN THE middle of the worn out city. I didn't ask why Miranda thought he'd successfully find his way to an ice cream shop 27 miles from his house in the middle of a huge city, but yes, I had my doubts.

Mrs. Ryan stayed in the car. Miranda told me to stay with her. I did. Watched Miranda's pink cast swing down the city sidewalks, her dark blue jean shorts hugging her hips. Simple faded yellow t-shirt down to her back pockets. Long brown hair between her shoulder blades, tossed in the summer breeze. A picture of beauty smashed between old historic buildings and dirty cement. Ashleigh brushed my mind like a cryptic breeze. She looked so different. I remember watching her walk away. Dark blue jeans too. Except she was taller with less hip and more up top. Fake, of course. Always a designer hand bag to match her shoes and necklace. One of five thousand. Her hips didn't sway as she walked. They jolted back and forth like a runway model with no training. She never seemed to rest. To just be. To wipe off the lipstick and live.

I forgot about Mrs. Ryan. She seemed to be as deep in thought as me. I turned the music down and relaxed. Looked at her. "Why do you think Max made Mr. Ryan like this?"

She looked up, then to her right, out the passengers window at a man smoking a pipe. "He always wanted things his way." She continued staring out the window as she spoke. "I just think life didn't turn out the way he imagined and he doesn't know how to handle it. He regrets a lot. He won't say it. And he won't change either. He just dwells in it."

"I can relate."

She finally made eye contact with me. "No, I don't think you can."

I didn't want to argue with her. People couldn't imagine Derek as David Bennett and I wasn't about to help her see my true colors. I nodded. Miranda tapped the hood of my car and came up to her mom. She leaned on the open window. "Have anymore envelopes in there?"

"Yeah. Why?"

She popped the glove compartment open and snatched an envelope, then hobbled her way back to the ice cream shop. A few seconds later she returned and sat in the back. "No Max, but there was a single mom in there who was trying to use food stamps to get her kids some ice cream. Hope you don't mind me using the envelope."

"Not at all." I turned the keys in the ignition. The engine rumbled. "That's what they're there for."

WE TRIED A FEW MORE PLACES. MRS. RYAN WANTED TO GO back home. We dropped her off and drove away. Miranda thought of one more place. An abandoned farm house in the middle of nowhere. Trees lined the driveway and circled around the house. Some windows had boards covering them, others looked worn but functional. The roof needed repair. Gutter hung from the left side like a cracked bone. The sun colored the sky orange behind the rolling hills and trees. We stepped out. Miranda linked her arm with mine and kept the crutches behind. I didn't mind. I helped her up the porch. The sign on the door said it was the state's property. Not to trespass. I looked at Miranda. She laughed. I pointed. She laughed again, then directed me to a window on the side of the huge porch. She tried to open it. When she failed, I did.

She sat on the sill and swung her cast over the window, like saddling up for a ride out west. I followed, looking around for cops.

"They won't arrest you. We'll just say we're looking for Max. We have a good excuse."

Right. Good thinking. We dodged missing floor boards and Miranda stopped at the fireplace, ran her fingers down the edges and swiped the dust from her hand. Ceilings were taller than two stories of most modern homes. Ornate design. Stained victorian wallpaper peeled from the walls. Beautiful. I imagined it restored. The fireplace lit and people crowded around it holding drinks and laughing. For a second I felt like Miranda. And laughed.

"What?" she said. Her eyes glistened in the fading sunlight.

I cupped her face with my hand and so badly wanted to kiss her. She swallowed. Couldn't tell if it was excitement or hesitancy, so I kissed her forehead and turned in a circle. "You think he's here?"

She hobbled to the doorway and motioned for me to follow. When I reached her she wrapped her arm around my back and leaned into my shoulder. I supported her with my right arm and we walked up the steps, checked every room, then heard something crack in the hallway.

A small closet. I opened it and peered up. "This goes to the roof."

She went up. The steps were small. Almost child-size. Felt like crawling through a tunnel. I followed her. She pushed the door at the top and revealed the moon. Sunsets never last long enough. She pulled herself out, then I did ... only to put myself right back in, away from the roof.

My hands trembled and my pulse throbbed in my ears. "I can't do heights."

She vanished from sight. Came back and whispered something I couldn't hear. Her smile looked super white against the dark blue sky. "He's up here. He's on the next level of the roof. Over that way by the chimney." She pointed to the left. "You need to help or I will have to with this cast." She knelt down and squinted her eyes. "Are you down there?"

I steadied myself on the shelf to my left. I couldn't move. My legs weighed a thousand pounds.

"Derek?" She sighed. "Please."

The edges of her face turned black. I closed my eyes. Opened them. It was no use. Everything was blurry. Spinning. And then blackness took over.

Everything disappeared.

Chapter Seventeen
Miranda

Pretty sure he fainted, but I couldn't tell. I peeked up at Max, still asleep on the roof with his favorite blanket. I didn't think I could hop up to that level. Not with my leg. I needed Derek. I needed him to get over his fear of heights.

I sat there for a minute. Wondering about my own fears and how crippling they became.

I climbed down to Derek. Rubbed his face. Smoothed his hair. The moonlight cast a blue tint on us. For a moment, I think my desires shifted. Looking at him there, so childlike in his blacked outness, I think I desired love. To love him and be loved by him, regardless of the possible rejection that could come one day. Maybe, I don't know, nothing seemed certain, but maybe it wasn't that I wanted to love him. Maybe I already did.

I kissed his brow down to his cheek, along his jaw, and stopped on his lips. Hovered there. My breath against his skin. His eyes twitched and fluttered, opened and closed. Something crashed and nature flashed a strobe light on us. Lightening. Max. I needed to get him quick. Storms scared him and made him run in circles, his palms against his ears. What if he ran off the roof?

Derek rose. Slow. Pulled himself up and crawled up the steps. I reminded him where we were, what we were doing, and what I needed him to do.

He sat at the top of the steps as I stood on the roof. His hands shivered in the warm summer night. I held them. Pressed them between my hands and looked in his eyes. "If you can't do this, I need to." Water collected in the corner of his left eye. Couldn't tell if it was a tear or not. I put his hands in his lap and turned to Max. Thunder blasted and lightening ripped open the sky. Max jumped from his sleep and stood, hands on his ears, terror on his face. The silent scream. He only did it when he was really, really scared. Looked like he was screaming but no sound escaped his gaping mouth. Eyes wide as cookies, he knelt and stood. Couldn't hear me calling his name. I ran to the other roof as fast as I could, given my casted leg. Pain shot through my hip and thigh. I kept going. No ladder in sight, I used my good leg to jump. Still couldn't reach the ledge and had no idea how Max did. He was shorter than me.

I jumped again and fell. "Max!" My screams competed with the thunder and nearly won. "Maxie, I'm here, bud. I'm here. Max!"

Derek appeared at my side. Every part of his body, ear lobes to finger-tips, quaked in the stormy night. Something out of a crazy movie. Not real life.

"Can you push me up there?" I said.

Derek shook his head and told me to sit down. I did. He placed one shaky hand on the ledge, then another. "One, two, three." He pulled his body weight and managed to get a knee on the next roof. Then the other. He disappeared. I stood back. Drizzles turned to buckets of water. I could barely see. Squinting, I saw movement on the other roof, but only Derek. Not Max.

My heart rate picked up. Rain drenched my clothes and I remembered. Max didn't like water. Freaked him out even worse than thunder. I paced in a circle with my head in my hands, hobbling.

Derek reappeared. I pretended not to notice what seemed to be a patch of pee on his jeans. And no, it wasn't from the rain. I could tell. Still a shaking mess, he handed me a soaked journal.

"Where is he?" I said over the thunder. Another shriek of lightening lit the sky. "Where's Max?"

Derek shook his head, trying to hold back tears. I hit his chest. "Where is he?"

He motioned to the door that led back to the attic. I climbed down, waited for him, and asked again.

"I didn't see him," he said. "I looked everywhere."

I composed myself. "Carry me."

"What?"

"As fast as you possibly can, get me downstairs and outside. If he fell"—I choked on my words, on the possibility—"if he's dying I don't want him to be alone."

Derek scooped me into his arms and raced down the big empty house. I could still feel his pulse throbbing a mile a minute. He set me down outside and ran the perimeter of the house. Came back a few seconds later. Alone.

"Where could he have gone?" I said. "We have to find him."

"Maybe we should call the cops. I'm not cut out for this."

"No. Cops will scare him even more. As if the rain and storm isn't enough." I reached for Derek's hand and squeezed. "When this is over we need to talk."

We went back inside. I motioned to the other side of the house. We walked up a different set of stairs from the kitchen to the second floor, then found another set of stairs at the end of the hallway. Once again, they led to a closet that seemed to go to the roof again. Maybe the part Max was on. Derek flung the closet door open.

Thunder cracked and peeled the sky again. I entered the closet and saw him. Rocking back and forth. Eyes closed. Forehead touching his knees like a recoiled caterpillar.

I touched his shoulder and exhaled. Relieved. Thankful. Exasperated. "Maxie, it's sissy."

He didn't move. Continued rocking like a caterpillar. I sat beside him and pulled his head to my chest, cradling my teenage baby brother. We sat in silence until the storm released it's grip from the earth. Derek reclined against the wall in the hallway, right outside the closet. I texted Matt. Told him to tell Mom I'd bring Max home within an hour.

Calmness settled in and I pulled Max's chin up, made him look at me. He avoided eye contact, but it was close enough.

"Max, honey." My eyes swelled with warmth. "I am so, so sorry for everything. I'm still your best friend. I love you. I am going to make it up to you."

He inched his cheek toward my lips. I kissed him. He reached into his pocket and pulled out a lollipop, twirled it in his hands, then moved it near my hand. I took it, thanked him, and led him to the car.

Derek followed. When we reached the car Max put one foot in and hesitated. I urged him to sit down. He pulled away and flapped his hands. I touched his shoulder and assured him it would be okay. We were taking him home. Tossing his arms in the air, he flung himself to the ground and thrashed his body into the earth.

Derek backed away. I knelt beside Max, crossed his arms over his chest, and held him on the ground until his tantrum subsided. A few minutes later he stood. My leg seared from my ankle to my sciatic nerve. Finally, I convinced him to sit in the car by telling him he could come home with me. In the car, I called Mom. Told her he'd be at my apartment and she could come over if she wanted. She said she'd meet me there.

Max never saw my apartment before and he doesn't do well with new places, but he walked right in and straight to my bedroom. I helped him into one of my old t-shirts and sweatpants. They fit him well enough. Couldn't get him to rest in my bed, so I streamed Curious George on my computer and tucked him under a blanket on the couch. Derek called Gavin and said he'd stay with me tonight, then took a shower and changed.

Mom called. "I'm here."

I buzzed the door and she walked in. Hair a mess. Face puffy. Tired eyes. She saw him on the couch and collapsed beside him. He looked passed her to the movie as she held his hand to her face, her body wrenching with deep sobs. I walked away. Back to my room. Back to Derek. He smelled like a crisp dew-dropped morning, but looked like a dehydrated plant.

He made himself comfortable on the floor, but I gave him the bed. I wanted to be near Max. We exchanged smiles. I grabbed Max's journal from my nightstand and went back to the living room. Mom cuddled with Max. Both already asleep. I sat at their feet and opened the journal. First few pages were torn out. Some had stick figure drawings. Then I finally found his voice again. Stacked in scattered magazine letters.

Home is not a place to me. Home is not a person to me. Home is not here. It is not with my father, my mother, my brothers, or my sister. I don't know what home is.

My sister taught me to plant. If the roots grew

strong, the plant would too. I don't know why I can't speak. My lips don't move when I ask them to. I want to tell them I can hear them fighting about me. I want them to know why I take my clothes off in public places and like stairs. They don't understand. No one understands. I'm not stupid. My roots must be weak.

The light switch is like life to me. I can't stop turning them on and off. Today it didn't work when the storm came. Mom said something about electric. I didn't understand. I needed the light switch to work. I needed it. Why didn't it work?

Someone moved the picture frame on my wall. I couldn't get it back to the right place. It hurt my head so bad I punched a hole in the wall. Dad and Mom are yelling. Dad hates me. I didn't do anything wrong. I don't know why he hates me. I try to love him, but my body doesn't let me. I'm sorry. My body doesn't do what I ask it to do. Sometimes it does the opposite.

You know that part in Ariel. I hear it a lot in my head. I want to be part of your world. That's what I say to people, but my lips don't move.

I closed the journal. Looked at Max. Amazed that he could communicate. After all these years he could, in some way, speak to the world around him. The words were sad, but I couldn't cry. Not knowing my brother could speak to me, albeit in slow torn letters pasted on paper. Smiling with the journal against my heart, I closed my eyes and allowed my mind to sweep me away to the land of dreams. The place where autistic children could move their lips and broken hearts were made whole.

Chapter Eighteen
Derek

Miranda sat across from me. Quiet and unable to stop smiling. Silverware clinked and clanged in the background. Waiters and waitresses flicked pens and carried trays, careful not to trip over the kids crawling under the tables and across the carpet.

Then I saw him.

I moved over so Miranda's head blocked his view of me. Last thing I needed was for him to see me. He sat with an air-brushed blonde. Typical. Some people never change.

I looked at Miranda. And some people change too much.

The waitress smacked her gum and knelt down, setting her elbows on the table. "What can I get you?"

"I will have creamed chipped beef with a side of home fries, two slices of French toast, extra syrup, three eggs lightly scrambled, a hot cup of water for tea, some cream, and a large orange juice." She thought for a second. "And a cranberry lemon muffin grilled with butter. Please."

The woman raised her eyebrows. I was used to Miranda's enormous appetite. Didn't phase me.

"I will have an omelette filled with home fries and onions, please." I handed the waitress our menus as she stood. "Thank you."

"That it?" she said.

I nodded. "She's the pig. I'm just a human."

Miranda laughed. So did the waitress as she disappeared around the mirrored wall.

"Hey, hey, look who it is." I knew the voice. Wished I didn't. I looked up as he pulled Blondie under his arm and squeezed her so forcefully she almost fell over.

I avoided eye contact.

"What brings you to Pennsylvania Dr. Bennett?"

I stood and excused myself. Went to the bathroom. Watched as Shawn and his girl walked away. Miranda smiled and nodded, then looked through the tables for my face. I ducked back into the bathroom, refreshed myself with cool water, then returned to her.

She didn't speak, but her eyes said everything. We ignored the obvious questions seated on the edge of her mind and the glowing frustration dangling off the edge of mine.

After we ate, she leaned on my shoulder as we walked to my car. "You know," she said. "I won't force you to tell me, but I won't stop myself from trying to snoop."

"Snoop what?"

"I want to know who Dr. Bennett is and what he has to do with Derek Rhodes."

Somehow I missed that. Didn't realize he said my name. My other name. I never did get used to being called that. Ashleigh always wondered why I never turned when she yelled, "David." She thought I was ignoring her and it only pissed her off even more. Good times.

"So?" Miranda said. "You gonna tell me or do I need to Google?"

I took Miranda back to her apartment without answering her question. She pat her cast. "I have an appointment with the doc today. We'll see how it goes." She glanced to her right at the passing strangers. The open window brushed her hair from her eyes. I reached for her shoulder, then stopped and put my hands back on the steering wheel.

She turned back to me. "Thank you."

"For what?"

"For overcoming your fears to save another person. For helping with my brother. For helping ... me." She squeezed my hand. "We'll always be friends, Derek. One day though, I think we'll be more like brother and sister."

"Why do you say that?"

She shook her head and put her hand on the door handle. "My heart isn't capable of true love." She pressed her palm against my heart. "And apparently, neither is yours."

I reached in my pocket and pulled out my wallet, then handed her my old license. The one that said I was a California resident named David Bennett. She took it and wrinkled her forehead.

"May help with your Google search."

Not a hundred percent sure, but I thought I saw her wipe away a tear. She hid it well, if so. I didn't know what to say. Had nothing to give. I wanted to fight for her, but this isn't how I envisioned it. I saw myself as the strong one. The man she wanted. But as much as I wanted to fight for the girl, I needed to battle myself first. And that meant I needed to see Ashleigh. One last time.

Miranda stepped out of the car and tapped the roof. I watched her until she faded from view. Something strange about this goodbye. I didn't like it. Especially knowing she'd soon be in the arms of another man.

I started the car, imagined her kissing someone else, then turned the car off and rang her doorbell. She buzzed me in. I hesitated, almost walked back to my car, then forced myself to walk up the stairs.

She opened the door. Tears all over her face. My heart twisted.

"Is it me?" I said, still in the doorway.

She took my hand and pulled me inside. We sat on the couch and she turned toward me.

"It's us," she said. "What are we doing?"

"Miranda." Something about her eyes made me weak. Made me lose my words and ability to say what I felt. I looked down. Tried to regather my thoughts. "Miranda, I ...."

"I want to know who you are. I want to know who David Bennett is." She tossed my license on to my lap. "And I want to know from your mouth. Not from Google's."

I shook my head. "It's not that easy."

"I'm not going to look it up. I feel like that's your easy way out of not expressing yourself and telling me the truth." She slapped my knee. "And after all the stunts you've pulled I'm pretty sure you don't deserve the easy way out either."

"You say I've helped you, Miranda, but how? You're trying to throw this all on me like I need to be saved when you haven't really changed at all."

She pulled back and crossed her arms. I closed my eyes.

"That's not true," she said. "And why do you have to be such a jerk?"

"Since when is honesty equal to being a jerk? I say these things because I love you."

The words stung us both like a bee. Love. I said it. Once the initial shock wore off we sat there, rubbing old wounds with our silence. Not sure about her, but I wondered why it hurt in the first place. Why it shocked. Why couldn't her and I be normal?

She stood and walked to the kitchen, clanked a few things around and returned with two cups of water. Ice and lemon in hers. Just lemon in mine. Exactly the way I liked it.

"I have changed," she said. "I feel more comfortable. I'm living more, allowing myself to feel things in places I never felt before. I'm nicer to my dad. My hair is brown. I mean, come on, my hair hasn't been brown in a seriously long time."

"But your heart is still on a shoestring." I flicked her laceless converse shoes. "And you still don't wear shoestrings."

She nodded.

"I don't know why I'm sitting here or why this has happened to me. After Ashleigh I swore off women. Swore off life. Decided to live alone and sulk in darkness for the rest of my life. I even considered ending my life. Ella invited me to her wedding and I knew I'd be the only family she had. So I picked myself off the couch and went. Then I saw you. I didn't think I'd fall in love with you, but I did. And yes, it freaks me out a little because you are highly unstable and emotionally revved up. I'm afraid of giving myself to you as much as you're afraid of giving yourself to me. I guess the difference is I am willing to find a stupid shoestring, loop it through my heart, and dangle it in front of your face. Unlike you, I see you as something, I mean, someone, worth the risk."

"I'm not unstable. That's just your perspective."

"Miranda, you can't sit still for two seconds. You're hair color may be the same, but your room color isn't. How many times have you repainted it since you've been home? You are not confident in who you are. Otherwise you'd know who you are and what you need in a man. Instead, you fling yourself at anyone who pines over you, then drop them on the curb when you get bored. You have no intentions of marrying them from the start.

You are a flirt and when real love is staring you right in the face you walk the other way because you're scared of what that might ask of you. You're afraid to sacrifice yourself. You don't want to give up your life the way it is, for who knows what reason."

She waited a few seconds to speak, then said, "You finished dissing me now?"

I stood. "How many times do I have to tell you? I'm not dissing you. I'm trying to love you, but you won't let me in. You'd rather play Cinderella with other guys." I walked to the door. "I'm sorry, Miranda. Sorry I even allowed myself to fall in love with you. It's obvious it will never work."

She walked over to me. "Derek, this may not make sense, but I'm letting you go right now because I love you more than I've ever loved anyone in my life. And although you like to blame every issue between us on my re-served heart, you're refusing to accept your own fault in this." She took my hand and put my palm against my chest. "This heart is not dangling in front of me. It's locked so deep down. I don't even know who you are, or who've you've been. You are locked up like a vault and I'm afraid no one has the key. You can blame me all you want, but I think you're the one who is still a little boy afraid to become a man."

She punched me with her words and it hurt. Mostly because it was true and no one ever said it before. What kind of man was I? After everything I did, I didn't feel like much of a man at all. Or a little boy. More like a monster. And if I wanted to win this woman's heart, she was right, I needed to kill the monster first. And it seemed damn near impossible.

I opened the door and kissed her cheek, until next time, I hoped. "Goodbye, Miranda."

I couldn't ask her to wait for me. I couldn't ask for anything. So, I left. When she closed the door I heard her slide down to the floor and sob. I stopped, considered going back in, but walked down the stairs instead. When I sat in my car I wiped my face and drove away.

Right to the Philadelphia International Airport.

Chapter Nineteen
Miranda

I pulled my legs to my chest on a lonely park bench in the middle of Philadelphia. Buildings towered above like glistening candles in the sky, mirroring the wispy clouds and jet planes above me. The sun, ready to warm the Pennsylvania terrain, spread it's golden fingers on the branches and sidewalks. A morning brushed with the sun. Businessmen and women bustled about. Brief cases tucked under their arms, ties choking their dreams, they rushed to their polished desks and stressful meetings. I didn't envy them.

Felt good to have my cast off. I rubbed my skin and watched an old woman hobble to the mailbox, kiss a small letter, and drop it into the blue bin. Something magical about letters, if you ask me. A hand-written note that takes time to write and time to ship. So much more beautiful than an email or a text. So much more romantic.

What did I know about romance anyway?

Oliver wanted to meet on Saturday. He insisted. I guess he wanted to prove his love for me after all these years. I didn't hold my breath. Beach flings never seemed to turn into substantial relationships.

"Miranda, is that you?" a voice said from behind me.

I turned.

"Where've you been?" Gilbert waved his wrinkled, dirty hand between us. "Haven't seen you for a while."

I patted the empty space beside me. "Sit down, Gilby. Stay a while."

He leaned onto his cane, took a few steps, then, after two minutes, managed to sit his butt on the bench. He leaned the cane against the side of the bench, sat back, and pulled the cuffs of his sleeves down over his wrists.

I opened my bag and handed him a turkey sandwich. He hesitated, then took it and bit into it with whatever teeth he had left.

"Maybe you should find her," I said, handing him a napkin and bottle of water. "You never know."

"I don't know how."

"I can help you."

He smiled. His gums shining in the summer morning. "You are the kindest lady I've ever known. My lady was a lot like you."

"Gilby, you made some mistakes, but it's not too late to go back and find your daughter. She may want to know you."

"Would you want to know your biological father if he was the reason your mother was murdered?" He sucked in the air and exhaled. "They took her away from me because I left her in the apartment alone while I went out to get high. What kind of girl wants to know the truth when it's that bad? I ain't trying to be ugly, Miss Miranda. Honest."

"Gilbert." I held his hand. "Your health is getting worse. You should find her. Do you really want to die on the streets? Alone?"

"You know how ridiculous these sidewalks are? I can't believe they don't put more money into getting these fixed up. Cracks and holes. I trip everywhere I go."

"Gilbert."

"These streets are all I've known for thirty six years. I ain't got it in me to leave it all behind."

I listened to him rant about the price of bread, the mean bus drivers with lead feet, and how good organic food is. Ever met a homeless man who refused to eat anything that wasn't organic? That's Gilbert. Good ole Gilby.

I watched him talk as boys and girls, men and women, walked by us, dotting life with their footprints. Poor Gilbert. Couldn't seek his only family. He truly believed the city streets and vacant stairwells had become his home. His family. Occasionally he pocketed enough money to stay in a hotel. When I could, I helped. Especially in the winter. But I wished I could do more. I wished he'd listen.

He glued himself to the past like frozen gum on the bottom of a park bench. Kind of like Derek. Kind of like ... me. I guess that's the common denominator between all broken souls. We're all stuck to dirty benches and afraid to pry ourselves away. Is it because the future is unknown, unpredictable? Or is it because the present is about as unflattering as the uniformitarian idea that the present is merely a key to the past?

Gilbert swigged the water and rambled as he limped away. Another homeless person wandering the land of plenty. Never quite made sense. I asked him to stay with me once, but he refused.

My phone rang. I picked up.

"Miranda, it's me," Heidi said. "Can you come over?"

"Why does it sound like you've been crying?"

"Can you come?"

SHE OPENED THE DOOR, THEN RAN UPSTAIRS TO GET RILEY. A few seconds later she returned, her daughter in tow.

"What's going on?" I said. "Thought it may have been Riley, but she looks fine."

Heidi sat on the couch and snuggled Riley beside her. I sat on the opposite couch, leaned forward, and motioned for her to spill the lima beans.

"It's Patrick."

"What? Is he okay?"

Her eyes were puffy and red. Hair a mess. Sparkly engagement ring on her left hand, missing. Something definitely happened and I couldn't imagine what.

Heidi clenched her jaw and held back tears. "It's my fault."

"What is? What happened?"

"I think I pushed him over the edge. After all he's done for me." Her lips trembled. "I pushed too far."

"You pushed what? You guys were doing so good. He proposed. You accepted. Both of you had enough stars in your eyes to fill the universe."

"Sometimes the universe is smaller than we think."

I shrugged. "What's that supposed to mean?"

She shook her head. "Nothing is ever normal for me."

I laughed. "Is life ever normal? For any of us? Life is filled with more drama than a Lifetime movie. Most people just ignore that. You ever think it's odd how people say a book is too unrealistic when it's actually softened

115

from reality so that people can digest it better? If I typed out my life story, word for word, including every detail around me, people wouldn't like it. Life is too real for fiction. People want to feel good all the time, but life is messy and sometimes it doesn't feel good. Like my neighbor who just committed suicide and the woman with four kids who crossed the street the other day and never made it to the other side. Not every story has a happy ending, so maybe you should change your definition of normal. To me? Normal is messy. Real. Ups and downs and in-betweens. I'm normal, weird as I may seem. And so are you. It's what we do with this mess that matters most."

"Well, you must've been writing again."

"Haven't in a few days. Just thinking. Wondering what to do with myself. Sometimes it's easier to sit here in the mess just because it's comfortable. But I'm starting to wonder if I stood up, drank some coffee, and found some inspiration, if I could turn this mess into a work of art."

"Do you ever speak like a normal human being?"

I smiled. "Oh, Heidi, Heidi, Heidi. Did you hear anything I said?"

"Kinda hard. You always speak in poetry or parables and I'm a simple person. Just say what you mean without all the science and art."

"I, my friend, am an old soul." Standing, I twirled around the room and Riley laughed. "And old souls appreciate when things are more complicated. Makes it worth figuring out. And when you figure it out, you'll realize the challenge was worth it."

She sighed. "Anyway, I got jealous. You know Pat has all these girls as friends. I get that. I know he's more sensitive than most men. He's a teddy bear kinda guy and girls go to him for advice. He's always been that and I don't want to take that away from him, but Nora texts him all the time. Sometimes when we're watching a movie. The worst part is he will ignore whatever we're doing and respond to her. I even catch him smiling and laughing at the phone and when I ask him to put it away, he gets defensive. Maybe I'm overreacting, like he thinks, but I see Gavin and Ella and after being married, pregnant, all that, he still refuses to look at his phone screen when she's in the room. Whether it's a man or a woman."

I sat beside her and put my arm around her. "Take a deep breath." She did. "Look, first of all, stop comparing anyone in the world to Gavin and

Ella. If we all did that we'd either end up better people or hopeless and suicidal, and since the better people thing sounds as far-fetched as they do, let's stick with comparing ourselves to normal people."

"I'm not sure I agree." She put Riley on the ground and reclined on the couch. "I think we should always compare ourselves to people who are better than us so that we are alway improving. Not in appearances or superficial stuff, but I don't know, I want to be a better person. If I compared myself to people who didn't challenge me I'd never grow."

"Okay, well, that's fine. Compare and contrast and grow, but you can't force that on Patrick. You need to love him regardless." I looked around the room. "Where's your ring?"

"Getting re-sized. Why?"

"Just wondering. You know, Derek refuses to change too. Somehow, I think, we managed to fall for each other, but it's weird. It's almost like we're too distracted with trying to change each other that we miss out on enjoying each other."

Heidi pondered my words. So did I. The silence between us vanished when the door opened. Patrick.

I stood. "I better get going."

"No, no." Patrick entered the living room and stood in front of Heidi. "I want you to hear this too. Perhaps you could benefit from it."

Oh, dear.

"I've spent a lot of time thinking." He took Heidi's hand. "I know things have been rough. We've been through a lot with Riley's surgery, Andy's parents, my parents, disapproval on every end. Obstacles upon obstacles. We've bypassed the honeymoon and somehow landed right in the crazy busy lifestyle estranged married couples struggle with and we're not even married yet." He looked at me. "Reese and I were just talking and he told me something. He says it every time he talks about Myra. He says, 'If it's not worth the struggle, then it's not a prize.'" His eyes darted back and forth, from his beloved to me to Riley. "Obstacles won't keep me from loving you, Heidi. And you're right about the phone thing. I'm sorry. I really am. There's a recurring theme all around us. Miranda, you and Derek are no exception. Sometimes the only obstacle that keeps us from loving others is ourself."

I swallowed and hung my thumbs on my belt loops. "My situation is a lot different than yours."

"No," he said. "It's really not."

"He's right," Heidi said, standing and wrapping her arms around Patty boy's waist. "You need to let go and move on. Grow into someone new. Allow yourself to experience real love for once."

"Hey." I faked a smile. "How'd this get turned on me?"

I walked to the door, opened it, and stood in the humid July afternoon.

"Where you going?" Heidi said.

"To show him he's not an obstacle and I'm officially done with being one myself."

Chapter Twenty
Derek

I stepped off the plane and walked down the terminal. Hands clenched, jaw tighter than a guitar string tuned by a five-year-old, I dialed her number and got no answer. She probably didn't recognize the number. I left a message. Told her we needed to talk. Truth is, I was making sure she still lived in Los Angeles. Yes, after I already landed there. Stupid, but I'm good at being irrational. More than Miranda might think. Or hope. Maybe even more than she'd approve of. Yes, in fact. Definitely more than she'd approve of.

I got myself a rental car and drove to her old place, knocked on the door, and seethed inside. Hate isn't a word I use often, but I'd grown so cold toward Ashleigh that I'm pretty sure it's the only word I applied to her. No, I didn't like it. I didn't want to hate anyone and that's why I found myself standing on her doorstep as a ripped dude in boxers opened the door. He scanned me up and down. I couldn't get passed his shaved and shiny pecs. What the hell?

He stepped outside and peered around. "Can I help you?"

"Does Ashleigh still live here?" I said.

"Yes." He sized me up again, like a butcher preparing the cow. "Who are you?"

"Derek Rhodes." I knew he wouldn't recognize the name. "She home?"

"No. She said she had to go take care of something work-related in Pennsylvania. She left this morning."

"In Pennsylvania?"

"I don't keep tabs on her, man." He stepped inside. "I'm her brother, not her pimp."

Nice. "Right. Thanks."

He shut the door and I walked away, back to the car. Pennsylvania? Now what?

Shawn.

Ashleigh went to Pennsylvania because of me. Shawn must've told her that he saw me at the diner. Great. What a waste of three hundred bucks.

I drove off and headed toward the beach. Reminded me of the time Ash and I flew to the East Coast to watch the sunrise over the Atlantic, then flew back home in time to see it set over the Pacific. Back when life was about fun and stupidity.

And not a lick more.

I LANDED IN VIRGINIA, GOT A RENTAL CAR, AND DROVE HOME. Time to move out of my apartment and plan for a place in The City of Love, as Miranda called it.

By the time I parked in front of my humble abode, the clock in the car said 8:28am. I rubbed my eyes, opened the front door, and walked up the stairs, down the hall, and saw her, slumped in front of my door, sleeping with her head on her designer hand bag. Long, blonde hair pulled back with that poofy top girls do. Reminded me of a poodle. Not a fan. I stood in front of her. She didn't budge. Her slender, flawless legs stuck out of her extremely short black dress like toothpicks. Her dress seemed more like a long shirt. A skintight long shirt.

Her eyes were closed, but I could still see the heavy eye makeup, as if the bright red lips and rosy cheeks weren't enough. Miranda wore a lot of makeup too, even blue and orange eye stuff, but something about it seemed more natural. Or maybe it was just Miranda.

She rustled and lifted her head. I offered her a hand. Half of me wanting to rip it off her arm, but it was time to be honest with myself. And her.

"How did you find me?" I said.

She stood in front of me and bent over to pick her scarlet red shoes off the ground. "Shawn said you were in Philly. So I went there. Then I got your call and it was a Virginia number. I was about to come home, but my brother called and said some guy named Derek Rhodes stopped by. I figured you would've changed your name after all that happened, so I looked up an address for Derek Rhodes in Virginia. There were only two. The first one wasn't you. So here I am."

I twisted the keys in the lock. "Surprised you figured all that out."

"I'm not as stupid as you think, David. Remember all the tests you cheated off of in college? That was me, you know."

"Book smarts are different than street smarts." I swung my arm toward the doorway. "Come in. We need to talk."

She stood next to the door as I closed it. Awkward silence.

"Want to sit?" I said.

A knock on the door. I turned and opened. Miranda panted, out of breath. "Derek, we need to talk. I'm sorry a thousand times. I realized you're right and I do love you. I wa—"

Ashleigh stepped into Miranda's view. Smirking. I shook my head and grabbed Miranda's hand. "It's not what you think. Come inside, please. I want you to hear what I need to say."

Miranda's eyes watered. "You have a prostitute here? I never would've thought."

"Ugh," Ashleigh shrieked. "I am not a prostitute."

"Miranda, I can explain. I need to explain. Please." But before I could finish my sentence she was down the steps.

Ashleigh laughed and rolled her eyes. "You gave me up for that?"

"I didn't give you up. The breakup was mutual and it was a good decision. Wait here." I ran down the steps and out the door. Miranda's car sped out of site, but I ran and caught up with her at the red light. She stared ahead, avoiding my eyes. I banged on the window, pleading her to open it and hear me out. Finally, the window cracked and she whispered through tears, "This is why I don't give my heart away."

The light turned green.

And she left.

ASHLEIGH FIDGETED ON MY COUCH. I WANTED TO KICK HER out, but not until I said what I needed to say.

She pulled a mirror out of her bag, smeared more lipstick on her lips, and pouted at the mirror. "Know why I'm here, David?"

I shook my head. "Don't really care, but I have something I need to say."

She batted her fake lashes. "Sure you don't want another fling before I leave?"

I stood so fast the blood rushed to my head. She crossed her legs, revealing more of her thighs. Boiling, I knelt down and flipped the coffee table, shattering glass all over the wood floor. She rolled her eyes and pouted in the mirror again. That's it. I couldn't take it anymore.

"Are you ever going to learn?" I yelled. Loud. From a deep place in the heart of a man that can only come out when every single button is pushed. And they were pushed. My circuits were fried. "I came after you not because I want you. Not because I ever wanted you. The only reason we even had what we had was because I was lost and you were pushy. It wasn't love. It wasn't even lust. Don't even know what the hell it was, but it was the worst time of my life and the only reason I wanted to talk to you was to tell you I was sorry. That I take the blame for what happened. I'm not saying this for you. I'm saying it for the girl who stole my heart. And after all that we've been through you want to flick your legs around and invite me into the place that's caused you so many issues so many times before? You haven't learned a thing. After everything, you still refuse to become a nice person." I picked up her hand bag and dropped it on her lap. "This ridiculous stuff that you waste your money on won't be going with you to the grave. It'll be taken to the nearest poor box and someone will sell it to make a little money. Such a waste of life."

"Don't be such an ass, David. I came here to give you something." She handed me a box and for the first time since I had known her she shed a tear. "I want you to have this and I want you to know something ... I haven't forgotten. Not a day passes. I named him after you." She walked to the door and wiped her face. "Maybe I'm still prissy and can't figure out how to be anyone other than who I am, maybe I'm a lot of things, but you don't know what I feel every day of my life. You aren't inside of me. I'm not as horrible as you like to think. That day changed my life. I still can't figure out if it's for better or worse, but it definitely changed me." One foot out the door, she turned. "And please, stop pretending to be such an asshole. You never fooled anyone."

She closed the door behind her. I sat on the couch, staring at the glass on the floor and the box in my hand, wincing.

It was small. Nowhere near heavy. And it rattled when I shook it.

I tried to open it, but stopped myself.

Chapter Twenty One
Miranda

The thing that really upset me . . . it wasn't the skimpy girl in his apartment or the look on his face when I caught him. And I appreciated his sprint to the red light, I really did. But he gave up. So easily. I sped off. He walked back to his house. Didn't get in his car. Didn't pick up his phone. No texts or calls. Maybe he had a good reason, but these are the things that made me want to retreat. Back to the place of fleeting romance and fugitive dreams. The place where my heart sat crammed away and out of reach. The place where I controlled how and when I felt pain.

Is that even healthy?

I needed ice cream. And cake. And brownies. And a root beer float. So I made them. Ella called when I sat down on my couch with my delightful collection of sugars. I didn't answer. She texted instead. *Miranda, hope all is well. Quick invite: Sarah is coming home in three weeks. Having a welcome back party at our house. Small and intimate. August 14 at 2pm. Bring my brother. I can't get ahold of him.*

I responded. *Where at?*

Ella: *Our house. Tylissa is moving in with family down south. Sarah is going to take one of the spare rooms for now. Just till her and James get married.*

Me: *Okay. I will be there. Not sure about your bro. We are in a rough spot.*

Ella: *What happened?*

Me: *I poured my heart out as Barbie stepped into view.*

Ella: *What's that mean?*

Me: *Nothing. No worries. I'm good. It will be okay.*

Ella: *I know he loves you. He has never been one to talk about it, but I can see it in his eyes.*

Me: *You see hearts in skulls and bones.*

Ella: *Love you, Miranda. :)*

She did love me. That I knew. Hard to imagine Ella doing anything less than loving. Her brother on the other hand? Yeah, not so sure about such things.

I stuffed my face with enough saturated fat to choke an army, then watched a romance movie for kicks. Is it just me or does everyone like to dwell in their heartbreak a little? Only seems fair. A broken heart deserves as much attention as a whole heart, maybe even more. A little sympathy, a dash of pity, a quarter cup of tears, a third of chick flicks, four cups of sugar, a good night of sleep, and the heart would be good as new.

A girl can dream, right?

OLIVER INSISTED ON PICKING ME UP FOR OUR DATE. I prettied myself up. Curled my hair, put on some natural brown eye shadow, peach blush, and sheer lipstick. After rummaging through my new wardrobe a thousand and three times I settled on a simple navy blue A-line dress with a flowing skirt. Soft, dainty, and somewhat 1950s. Right before leaving I slipped on a pair of two-inch white sandals and wrapped a white scarf around my head so it accented my hair and flowed down my back.

Oliver rang the door. I buzzed him in and met him downstairs. His jaw dropped when I reached the end of the stairs. I held the railing, stood there, smiling and admiring his midnight blue eyes. He remained speechless. I let go of the railing and stood in front of him. "You look older." I touched his jaw. "Facial hair?"

"And you aren't a girl anymore." His British accent weakened everything in me.

"Ten years does that to a person. Although I'm starting to relate to that Britney Spears song where she claims she's not a girl, but not yet a woman."

"No," he said. "You're definitely a woman."

We drove to a nice restaurant, his choice, and the waitress led us to a table outside by a water fountain and a nice garden. Reminded me of Derek.

We ordered. I didn't overwhelm him by ordering too much. Kept it simple. The food came during our light catch up conversation about school, dumb stuff, and Max's recent ordeal.

We talked and laughed our way through dinner and finally set our forks on our empty plates. He stared across the table at me. I stared back. We leaned into each other, ordered desert, and twisted the conversation knob to a deeper level.

"Do you think we can be together?" he said. "Because ... I don't know. I think, perhaps, I mean, I don't know, but I think perhaps I love you even more than I did that first day."

I smiled. Normally I'd soak it up, flirt back, oogle ogle and lovey dovey grovel, but I couldn't muster it up this time. So I smiled. Just smiled.

"I don't mean to. It wasn't my intention. I don't want to seem strange." He smoothed the napkin over his plate. "It's just I can't stop thinking about you."

"Oliver, dear." I shook my head. "You barely know me."

"You can't deny what we have."

I laughed. "Please enlighten me. What exactly do we have?"

"Well, you know."

"Are you lonely?"

"It's not that."

"Okay, you are gorgeous. No doubt about that. You're sweet. You're funny, from what I know at least. But these things are all a dime a dozen. In fact, there are plenty of amazing fish in the sea and at first glance they all seem the same, but they're not."

He tilted his head. "What makes them different?"

"Science."

"Science?"

"That which repels also attracts. Like a magnetic force." I smiled. "I'm afraid, without my consent, my heart has been stolen. I'm still in shock myself. It's rather alarming, actually. I don't know if I'll ever understand how this happened, but I think I'm going to allow it to be what it is. I'm really sorry. You are wonderful and something tells me I might regret this, but the truth is my heart is somewhere else and until I get it back, if I do, I'm quite simply not the girl for you."

"You mean woman."

"Sure." I laughed. "Woman."

My phone buzzed. Derek called. Left a voicemail. Interesting timing.

Oliver took me home. I kissed him on the cheek, wished him luck, and walked to my favorite city bench. The one on the brick sidewalk under the trees. Their branches reached across the road, entwined in a loose embrace. A canopy of bark over the quiet street. Electric candles lit the windows across the street as a child pulled the curtains until Mama Bear lifted her up with one hand and disappeared behind the fabric. Life. That's why I sat on park benches. In bad times, it helped me realize things weren't so bad. In good times, it helped me appreciate them even more. I'd sit there for hours sometimes, watching life around me, realizing that there's so much more to this life than me.

The July heat, albeit nighttime, suffocated me. My shirt was already sticking to my chest. I pulled it away, blew air on my skin, and reclined on the bench, staring at the stars through the tree branches.

After a few minutes, I listened to my voicemail. "Miranda, it was just Ashleigh. I didn't even kiss her hand, much less anything else. Almost ripped her hair right out of her head, but that's another story. And no, I'm not serious. You know I wouldn't do that for real. Anyway, there's some stuff I need to tell you. It's time. I'm ready. Call me back, please."

I wasn't ready to call. Yet. So I sent a quick text. *Meet me at my parents house next Saturday. Having the family over to spend time with Max. We can talk after. Until then, I need some time to think.*

He responded. *Why their house? I want to talk first.*

Me: *Because. I want to stare at you across the room and see if I can stand being in the same room with you and not touching or talking. If the magnets attract, we can talk. If they repel, let's walk away and forget it ever happened.*

Derek: *I'll never forget you, Lizzy.*

Me: *Coming?*

Derek: *Ok.*

"IT'S JUST A LITTLE GATHERING FOR MY FAMILY," I SAID TO myself as I stared at my small wardrobe. Maybe he would like me dressed like Barbie, I thought, but didn't own anything of the sort and I'm not sure I wanted to. What would he find most pretty?

I tried on different outfits and settled with the most normal thing I owned. A pair of skinny jeans and a black t-shirt. I didn't straighten my hair or curl it, which meant it looked a little frizzy with a slight wave. And low and behold, the biggest shock of all, no makeup. Not even lip gloss.

I blinked at myself in the full length mirror that hung on my closet door. Kinda liked being normal. It seemed so . . . normal. So ... real. He always said he liked a woman at rest. Well, I guess this would be Miranda at rest.

My pink converse shoes, laceless, stood out to me. I put them on and decided to surprise Derek with a gift.

I grabbed some paper, cut out a heart, and in my neatest, fanciest hand-writing I wrote him a note. My Gift to You. Then I drove to Walgreens, got a red shoe string, and sat in my car stringing it through the pink heart. "There." I held it up against the sun. "Perfect."

I placed it into the pocket of my purse and drove away. When I arrived at the house Matt greeted me at the door. I looked around for Derek and my pulse picked up. He wasn't there yet.

I gave Lydia a hug and she handed me my little nephew. So adorable. I pressed his cheek against mine and kissed his tiny fingers, then handed him back to his mama. "How old is he now?"

She plopped him back into her wrap. "Almost three months." His fingers curled around hers. "He is growing so fast. I already want a newborn again."

I laughed. "Wow. I guess labor wasn't that bad, huh?"

"It was. But it was also worth it." She moved the living room curtains and peeked out the window. "Oh, look. That's so cute."

I glanced out to the front lawn as Mom walked over to me. She hurried back to Max in the dining room and took his hand. "Look, Max. It's Steve from Blue's Clues."

Max's favorite. Steve jogged down the path with a small Blue's Clue's stuffed animal under his right arm and giant salt and pepper shakers under his left arm. He knocked on the door, but Max was already opening it, jumping up and down, and squealing with glee.

Matt looked at me and smiled. "How much did you pay him to do this?"

I looked over my shoulder. "Me? I didn't pay for it."

Steve walked in. Our eyes met. My smile pulled my face apart and I couldn't help but laugh. Bent over in hysterics, I nearly collapsed on the floor. Steve put one hand on Max's shoulder. "Now, we gotta find the first paw print. You know what to do. Let's put on our thinking caps and think, think, think." He put a birthday hat on Max's head and surprisingly Max kept it on.

I walked over to him, unable to hide my grin. Matt stepped between us, put one hand on Derek's shoulder and the other on mine, then eyed us both up and down.

"You know," he said. "You guys are like an odd Danny and Sandy."

I smiled. "What?"

"Look at you, trying to be all plain Jane for Derek while he went out and got all weird for you." He tapped our backs. "You're all I need. Oh, yes indeed."

He walked away singing *Grease* songs as I held Derek's hand and mouthed, "Thank you."

"I never meant to change you, Lizzy." He gave me a stuffed pepper shaker. "I like your colorful way of viewing life. I didn't want to dilute you. Only wanted to filter out the dirt and help you live and rest in who you are and not who you want to be. Or who anyone else wants you to be."

"I'm sorry," I said. "I wanted to fix you. I really did. I have a complex or something. Can I just enjoy you now?"

He nodded and took a seat next to my brother on the couch. A simple family party. Nothing more. Dad never came out of his bedroom. Only the distant sound of a baseball game playing in the house told me that he was home, watching television as usual.

"Michael coming?" I said to Matt.

"Does Michael ever come? I was surprised he even showed up for my wedding."

"Barely," Lydia said. "Something wasn't right with him."

I shrugged. "He's extremely introverted and leans phlegmatic. What's normal for him seems anti-social to us. He's always been that way."

Lydia nodded, but she had no idea what I was talking about. Matt nodded too, as he sipped on a freshly squeezed strawberry lemonade. He knew what I meant. Our oldest brother always seemed aloof. Like he didn't care. Like my dad. But I believe he cared a lot. Only problem is he never learned how to express it. So he kept his distance.

I watched Derek across the room, sitting at the dining room table drawing pictures with Max. I couldn't wait to scoop him away and give him the heart I made. Finally tell him how ready I was to be his.

Dad walked down the steps, looked around the room emotionless, grabbed a beer from the kitchen, and staggered into the dining room. Mom stood, as she always did when he entered the room. And it wasn't a sign of respect and honor.

He walked behind Max, squinted his eyes at Derek, and set his beer on the table in front of Max. "Drink it." When Max didn't respond he shoved his shoulder blade and repeated. "Drink it." Max stopped coloring Magenta and Blue and twiddled his thumbs. The color drained from Derek's face and I didn't want to see what he'd provoke my father to do.

I nudged Matt. "He's drunk. Stop him before something happens."

Matt sat forward and whispered, "I don't know what to do. I'll just make it worse. Ignore him, he'll go back to the television in a few."

I wasn't so sure.

Mom refused to speak up. She wrapped one arm around her stomach and bit her nails on the other hand. Dad picked the bottle up and forced it to Max's mouth.

Derek pushed his chair back and stood. "Sir."

Max wound his thumbs around each other a mile a minute as Dad poured beer down his face. I ran to his room and came back with a new shirt before he flipped out. Dad stepped away from Max and toward Derek. I helped Max take his wet shirt off and put on the new one. His eyes darted around the room. Soon, he'd be in a full blown tantrum.

Derek didn't back away when Dad pushed his shoulder.

"I'm not scared of you, sir." Derek's eyes never blinked. "I'm not scared of you because the person I am is so much worse than you. You're not angry or bitter, you're just a mess." He motioned toward Max. "You say all this nonsense about wishing your kid was never born, well, let me tell you something."

"I don't think I asked for your opinion." Dad's indignant eyes made me shrink.

"Then you can leave the room while I tell your daughter why she deserves better than you ... and me." Derek looked at me while he spoke. "When I was in school I chased a girl. Stupid. She went to med school and I followed. We both became gynecologists. She was asked to be a part of a local clinic. Money was amazing. I was offered a position at the same place. Took it. Didn't think anything of it. We were helping women who were raped. Women who had babies with deformities or Down syndrome and were counseled into believing the child would be better off killed. Teenagers with missing boyfriends and ashamed parents. Women who thought their lives were in jeopardy because of their pregnancy. That's what I told myself anyway. That's what everyone was made to believe. We were doctors like everyone else. Helping people live better lives."

His hands shook violently as he braced himself on the chair. He looked back to Dad, then to Mom, then back to me. "I can't tell you how many babies I murdered when the mother ended up weeping on the floor while her man stood there, unfeeling like you." He looked at Dad, who was staring right at him, listening . . . oddly enough. My heart thumped in my ears. I wiped my palms on my jeans and stepped toward Derek. I reached for his hand, but he jerked away.

"I would stand there at the edge of this bed in a sterile room," he continued. "White walls. Beeping machines. And I'd dig around inside these women with a suction curette." His tone deepened and loudened all at the same time. "The stuff I've seen and done . . . ." He shook his head and raised his voice. "You should be ashamed of yourself." He pointed at Dad. "Here you are wishing your child was never born, treating him like a piece of trash. You're no better than me. You're not shoving scissors into the skulls of little babies and pulling off their limbs, but you're killing your baby in other ways, ripping him apart."

Dad walked out of the room. Max left long ago. No idea when, I didn't notice. I reached for Derek. He let me hold his arm.

"We were trained not to call them babies," he said to the rest of the gaping mouths and wide eyes. "But I know better now. I'd have blood all over me as I tried to put together pieces of these little babies. They looked like people. Little tiny people. Arms, legs, heads. Some of them even sucked their thumbs. I could tell when I had to do an ultrasound for some women. We needed to make sure we got it all out of the woman." He swallowed hard. Glassy and red, his eyes shined in the light coming through the window. "So sometimes we used the ultrasound. Either way, my gloves would be covered in blood as I counted limbs and body parts. The worst part was that some of them were born alive."

He coughed away his tears and lashed out at himself, throwing his arms back and almost knocking the chandelier off the ceiling. "There are some people . . . people like me . . . who don't deserve forgiveness." He looked at me. "Much less love."

I tried to wipe the bitter tears from his face, but he pushed me away and walked to his car. I stood with Matt and Lydia as he sped from the house and down the street. Matt looked at me. I didn't know what to say. What do you say to that? Apparently, none of us knew. So we stood there in silence until I mustered the strength to say goodbye to Max and go after Derek.

Chapter Twenty Two
Derek

I pulled over. Couldn't see straight. Didn't know where I was. I left Miranda's family and drove. No destination. Hot, angry tears on my face. Tears I held back for years. I didn't allow many to fall, until the car rolled to a stop and into park.

Miranda called, asked if I was okay. Unfortunately, although thousands of lives were taken by my own hand, I was okay.

I hated being okay.

"That's not the worst," I said. "Miranda, please don't hate me."

I set the phone on speaker, put it on my dashboard, and recalled the worst day of my life.

HIS TINY FACE HAUNTED ME. IN MY DREAMS AND WHEN I woke up. The rubbing alcohol scent filled the room as I pulled him out of Ashleigh only to find him alive. Still breathing. It happened a few times. Rare. It wasn't supposed to happen with my own child.

She lied. Said she cheated on me and I was the only person she trusted to abort the baby. I'd already done thousands upon thousands of abortions. Clean and legal. Neighboring communities considered me a master. I made enough money to earn the title and was on the verge of starting my own "Family Planning Clinic."

When I pulled him out of her he was older than she thought. Weighed just over two pounds and looked . . . real. I tried not to look at him as I set him in a tray across the room. His arms flapped above him like they do in the ultrasounds when they are still inside their mother. I ignored the arms. Wasn't sure what to do or if I wanted to acknowledge that he was aborted alive. The nurse cleared her throat a few times as I finished cleaning up Ashleigh's cervix and finalizing the procedure. His arms and legs flailed behind me. I could see the reflection in the metal of my "surgical instruments." The nurse tried to ignore his slight, barely audible whimpers. His moving, grasping for life limbs. His lungs were not yet fully developed. He needed oxygen. He needed help. My boss entered. A bone-chilling man as arid as the room. Considered abortion a completely healthy way to make money and went to great lengths to preserve his "practice." I believed him. Agreed with him. He saw the baby and flipped him into a bucket on the floor by the sink, then tightened the lid.

"Sir," I said. "Isn't it the law to try and save the child when the abortion fails?"

The nurse excused herself as Dr. Thompson kicked the bucket. "Have you ever seen what happens to one of these things when it gets taken to a hospital? Well, at least the one I worked at." He stretched a glove over his hand and snapped it at his wrist. "Same thing, David. They leave it there to die while they go on taking care of the babies people actually want. Remember, I used to work at a hospital before this. I've seen it myself. This is our job, don't let emotions get in the way." He smiled. "Besides, Dr. Bennett, abortions never fail here."

Ashleigh opened her eyes. Still out of it, but more alert and aware. She looked at me for reassurance. I shrugged. She tried to thrust her body off the table. I held her down. Dr. Thompson assisted.

The baby in the bucket. I couldn't stop thinking about it. I wish I could lie and tell you that I actually believed Ashleigh, but I didn't. I knew from the start I was aborting my own flesh and blood. I didn't want to be tied to Ashleigh forever. Didn't want that life. So instead, I tried to suck the life out of my son and traded what I believed would be a better life for hell on earth. I aborted so many other babies. What would be the difference if it were my own? We were trained to see it as a job, as an "it," a "thing," not as a person. My son was not a person. He was a fetus. A fetus who would make my life more complicated. That's what I should've believed, but....

I couldn't take it. I left Ashleigh with Dr. Thompson, grabbed my son from the bucket as he gasped for air, his skin raw and burned in places from the chemicals I injected before. I wrapped him in a hospital gown that quickly turned red and rushed him to my car, holding him on my lap as I sped to the hospital.

He stopped breathing right before I got out of the car. His small face crinkled as I sprinted inside and up the stairs. I guess with my uniform and the fact that I was well acquainted with the folks there, they didn't say anything. Or maybe it was the bloody infant in the towel. I finally found who I needed. Some of them were even my "friends." I told them what happened, but didn't tell them the baby was my own. Explained the failed abortion and begged for help, but Dr. Thompson was right. No matter how much I screamed and pleaded for someone to help the limp child in my arms, there wasn't an urgency for a child suffering from an abortionist's hands. Unwanted. Discarded. Fragments of what could have been. Nothing more than a heap of trash ready for Monday's big green truck to hull away.

That's all these kids were.

I held his lifeless body. Analyzed his long fingers and full lips. His dark brown hair and bruised head. He reminded me of my baby pictures. Images scorched me. Images that could never be. His first steps and first cake-smothered birthday. The time I'd scare off his girlfriends and teach him to drive a stick. The life that could never be. The life I ended. The life I wanted, but it was too late.

Ashleigh and I had a private funeral. Buried him with a real stone and everything. I refused to be a "doctor" from that point on.

I realized there's a fine line between helping people and hurting people and I wasn't sure I was the man to help anyone heal. Not after that.

I HELD MY BREATH AS I AWAITED MIRANDA'S REPLY. SHE sniffed, waited, then said, "Meet me at the park bench by my apartment in fifteen."

She hung up. Wasn't the response I hoped for, though I'm not sure I remember hoping for any response. I shifted the car into drive and a paper caught my eye, flapping in the breeze under my windshield wipers. I put the car in park, grabbed it, and sat back down.

There, on a tattered piece of green construction paper, twenty six letters ripped out of a magazine spelled something so simple, yet so profound, considering the person who wrote it.

They will forgive you if you ask.

I WAITED FOR MIRANDA ON HER FAVORITE PARK BENCH AS the August day began to settle into night. My past, finally exposed, made me feel naked. And that made me nervous. I loved Miranda. She fascinated me from day one, but I didn't know I loved her. Not right away. Sometimes she irritated me like crazy, but those times seemed to be far less now. Perhaps it was me. Perhaps she softened the hardest parts of me. Something no woman ever tried to do. No one cared enough.

Silky hands covered my eyes. I held them, brought them to my lips, and kissed them. She sat beside me. Her eyes sparkling in the last of the sun. She'd been crying.

"Thank you," I said.

She sniffed. "For what?"

"For not hating me."

"Is that why you refused to kill mosquitos?"

I nodded.

"And the money?"

I nodded again.

"How much did you make?"

"A lot. It's a five-hundred billion dollar business." I handed her the box Ashleigh gave me. "Look at this."

She opened it and pulled out the tiny piece of plaster with a mini footprint on one side and a handprint on the other. Miranda's eyes glistened as she looked at me. "Did you name him?"

I shook my head. "Not officially. Ashleigh did though." I handed her his death certificate wrapped up in his birth certificate. "She had them made. I never knew until I opened this box." She read the name as I read aloud. "Derek Thomas Rhodes Jr." I tried to force my hands to stop shaking. "Killed by his own father."

Miranda took my hand into hers. "Who you were then is not who you are right now. We all change." She tried to laugh. "I'm proof. I'm not going to lighten what you did because we both know it's as horrible as it sounds, but Derek...." She placed the back of my hand against her cheek and hung her head. "This doesn't define you. Just like my clothes and hair don't define me. You're a new person. You have to let go."

I ran my index finger along her cheek. "How do I let go of the thousands of lives I've stolen? How do I go on living and allowing myself to love and be loved when I helped steal the chance from so many others? Thousands, Miranda. I don't deserve to live."

"Is that why you planted all those flowers?"

I nodded. "One for each abortion."

She squeezed my knee and leaned in. Centimeters from my face she whispered, "Live for them."

"When someone murders another human being, they go to jail. People don't consider abortion murder. They consider it a normal and practical option for women who, for whatever reason, don't want their baby. I'll never forget the abortion I did for a young mentally handicapped girl who was raped. Her parents and my boss, we all agreed it was the best option. So we made the decision for her and I left my office feeling proud that day. Honestly thought I was helping people. That's what I believed, but after seeing my son take his last breath I can tell you this ... I deserve life in prison." I exhaled, looked around at the people walking by, the birds flapping from tree to tree, and the squirrels scurrying up the electric poles. "Only the world doesn't agree with me, so I've had to create my own prison. Who am I to say I deserve to live when for so long I believed those babies were embryos devoid of life? Little things, not children, that didn't deserve a chance. My own son, Miranda, my own son..." I looked at her as my eyes stung with pain. "All because I didn't want to be tied to Ashleigh."

"When is his birthday?"

"March 22nd. He would be three years old next spring." I stood. "Anyway, here I am."

She stood in front of me and searched my face. I let her.

"I love you, Lizzy." I brushed her hair behind her ear. "But I have to be honest, I fear having children. I don't know if I can and I can't ask that of you."

"Whoa, whoa, don't jump too far ahead. I refuse to speak of children until there's a ring on my finger, and you know how difficult it would be for me to allow someone to slip a ring on this finger."

I smiled. "How reassuring."

She rocked on her heels and smirked up at me. "I'm glad I know you. All of you."

Yes. I was too. Felt good to come out of my shell and feel the warmth of life on my skin again, albeit painfully hot compared to the hypothermic life I was used to. She reached into her pocket and handed me a piece of pink construction paper shaped like a heart with a red shoe string looped through it. I turned it over in my hands and read her note.

My Gift to You.

My chest throbbed with a feeling I'd never felt before. A feeling I can't describe.

She smiled and wrapped her arms under mine and around my back, then looked up at me. "Let me love you."

"Only if you let me love you."

She leaned her lips close to mine. "Someone once told me that you know you've found the right one when both people feel like they don't deserve each other." She closed her eyes, then leaned back and looked at me. "Let's love each other because we can't help it, not because we deserve it."

"The magnetic force is unstoppable, I guess."

"I don't guess. I know."

She laid the paper heart against my chest and kissed me. Her gentle, soft lips on mine. I pulled her into me and kissed her back. And somehow, at some point in the midst of that kiss, I became a man.

They say two people become one when they get married. I don't know. All I know is that kiss and that paper heart on a shoestring made me feel whole for the first time in my life. And that wholeness took me from my cowardice boyhood to a manhood I couldn't deny. The best part of me, the part of me I needed, lived inside the little woman in my arms.

My true and honest better half.

Chapter Twenty Three
Miranda

We held hands all the way to Lancaster for Sarah's welcome home party. Ella opened the door and gave me the biggest hug I think I'd ever experienced in my life. Well, as big as possible considering her pregnant belly. She scooted toward Derek and wrapped her arms around him too. "So glad you guys are finally together. I watched you hold hands from the car to the house." She hugged me again. "I'm just so happy for you two."

Gavin touched her belly from behind. "You sure you're okay?"

She nodded. "Come in, come in. Sarah should be here soon. Want to see the room I made for her?"

We followed her up the creaky wood stairs and down the long hallway. She opened a bedroom door. Slivers of light danced on the floor and the white-clothed bed. Ella pointed to the art on the walls. "These are all photographs she took. And this"—she stopped in front of a beautiful portrait of a blonde woman in a field, her back to the artist—"is a painting Gavin recently made of her." The room was bright and happy. A book shelf filled to the brim with books and picture frames of Sarah's friends and family. A closet overflowing with clothes. And a neatly wrapped gift on the bed next to a bowl of candies.

Ella touched the candy. "I made these. Since Sarah's cancer scare she refuses to eat sugar. So these are her favorite chocolate candies made with stevia. Took my forever to get it right."

Derek smiled and put his arm around her. "You're a good friend. No doubt about it."

She tapped his chest. "What about a good sister?"

"Eh, debatable."

She smiled. "Thank you for telling me about your past. Your baby." She held her stomach. "I can't imagine, but I'm here for you. And I love you."

"I think I hear Matt downstairs," he said, and walked out of the room.

"What you're doing for Sarah is beautiful," I said. "It really is."

"I'm not doing anything more than any other person would do."

"And thank you for always believing in Derek. He's been through a lot, but I've seen a change in him since he let the truth out. I think it even changed my dad. For the first time in my entire life he called me just to ask how I was doing. I thought someone paid him to do it."

She winced and leaned on the bed.

"Are you okay?"

"Yeah," she said. "Braxton Hicks contractions. Nothing serious yet. Let's go downstairs. Don't want to miss Sarah."

We walked down the steps. I noticed Ella walked much slower down them than when she walked up a few minutes before. She went over to Gavin by the front door. I hugged Matt and Lydia, kissed the little one, and pulled Derek aside. "Is Ella in labor?"

"Huh? How am I supposed to know?"

"Weren't you trained in this stuff?"

"Well, yeah. That's what I was going to do originally, but I don't know. She seems fine to me."

"She's kinda waddling and walking slow."

"If she was in labor, we'd know it. Women in labor don't walk around their houses entertaining guests."

He had a point. A few seconds later everyone stood on the big wrap-around porch as James and Abby escorted Sarah up to the house. She didn't look as bad as I imagined, but definitely not her old self. The left side of her face was mostly scarred, including the skin around her eye and lips. Each step she took was labored and deliberate. From a distance, she could've been mistaken for her old self. But there was no mistaking the enormous smile stretched across her face.

Tears in her eyes, she embraced Ella, then looked around at the rest of us. "Thank you all for doing this. I'm so thankful to be home."

My eyes filled up. She hugged Gavin, then Matt, Lydia, Dee, and her cousin Cheyenne. Finally she made her way to Derek and me.

"Look at you two." She smiled and hugged me. "You look so good together."

Derek hugged her. "You've always been another sister to me, even though I've been distant the last few years. I'm so glad you're okay."

"It hurts a lot." She leaned back into James for support. "Still a lot of pain and I'll need more work done."

"Come inside," Ella said to everyone. "Sarah, your parents said they'll be here a little late. They got stuck in traffic."

Ella beamed as she led Sarah and James into the house. Abby, James' little girl, followed behind. I tapped her on the shoulder. "Doing okay there, little lady?"

She looked up at me and half-smiled. "Yeah. Daddy says now that Ms. Sarah is back I will get to see her more."

I smiled. We all sat in the living room talking as though none of us ever suffered. Everyone laughed and joked like friends do. The beauty of true friends, I thought. Ups and downs are all the same with friends like this. Almost as though the love is so much stronger than the circumstances that it melts the good and the bad into one big ball of life to be savored, together.

At some point in our conversations, someone screamed upstairs and Gavin dropped his glass of water all over the living room floor and ran up the steps. I scanned the room. Ella was the only one missing.

Before any of us could react, Gavin ran back down the stairs. "Derek, I need your help."

"Me?" Derek said.

"You're the only doctor here. Get up here." He ran back up the steps.

Everyone stared at Derek. I nudged him. He gave me the what-am-I-supposed-to-do look.

"She's your sister, Derek," I said. "Go."

He kissed my cheek and whispered in my ear, "I love you."

I smiled as he jogged up the stairs, then stopped and motioned for me to follow. We found Ella in their bedroom. She arched her body like a rainbow and scrunched her face in pain. After a few seconds she looked at us.

"I was trying to hold off for Sarah. My contractions got really bad in the last two hours and then while everyone was talking downstairs I came up here and the contractions got really intense. I was trying to hide it, thinking they'd pass. I don't think the baby wants to wait." She sat on the edge of the bed and braced herself.

"We need to get you to the hospital," Derek said.

Gavin knelt on the ground beside her and held her calves. "We called the midwife. Ella was planning on giving birth at a local birth center. Midwife said all the pressure and pain she's having means she's too close to get in the car. So she's on her way here, but there's a ton of traffic on Route 30 right now and she's stuck in it."

Ella arched her back again and screamed.

Gavin stood, helpless. "What can I do, love?"

She shoved his arms away and reached for a pillow, then squeezed it as hard as she could.

I sat beside her. "Ella, dear, try to stay calm. I'm sure your midwife will be here soon. We'll help you until then."

She rode out another contraction. Derek stood in the doorway, pale as a snowy morning. Gavin and I helped Ella get on her side on the bed, but the next contraction threw her into a frenzy and she ended up on all fours on the bed.

"The pressure," she yelled. "It's too much pressure."

Gavin moved her skirt and peeked inside. "Oh, no. Oh, no, no, no. What do we do?" He grabbed Derek. "Do something. I see blood."

Derek swallowed so hard his entire chest quaked. He helped Ella roll onto her side, then her back, and asked me to take her underwear off and roll her skirt up. I did. He spread her legs and looked at Gavin. "That's not blood, man. That's your daughters head." He tapped my hand. "Get me towels. Tons of them."

Derek's hand trembled as he placed it on the baby's head. "Ella, push, nice and long, with your next contraction."

"I can't." She screamed and cried as she twisted her arms behind her and gripped the headboard. "It hurts so bad. I can't do it."

Gavin sat beside her and looked to Derek for reassurance. They nodded to each other, which made me feel better. I gave Derek the towels and he managed to slip them under Ella during her next contraction. She closed her legs and lifted her body up, moaning in pain. If Derek ever wanted children, I think I definitely wanted the epidural.

Gavin held her right leg and I held her left. During her next contraction Derek told her to push. She squeezed Gavin's hand until it turned red and pushed. The baby's head looked like a bowling ball inside of her. I couldn't imagine it coming out. Next contraction, she pushed again. The head came out along with a little blue face. I held my mouth and cried. Ella relaxed and sighed. "Is she out?"

"Her head is out." Derek held the head in his right hand. "Next contraction, I want you to push again. Her shoulders will come out next then she'll slip right out."

Ella squeezed Gavin's hand again. "It hurts so bad. I can't push again."

"You're doing good, love. One more push. Try one more time."

She lifted her back and bore down again. A shoulder popped out. Ella screamed and pushed again. Another shoulder.

"Almost there." Derek held the baby in both hands under her shoulders. "One more."

She closed her eyes and pushed with everything left in her. Adelaide slipped into the world. Right into Derek's arms. Ella flopped back on the pillows, crying and kissing Gavin. My eyes were on my love, hugging the infant to his chest, blood all over his shirt, and tears streaming down his face as he smiled uncontrollably. Ella smiled as Derek kissed the new life in his hands, pressed his cheek against hers, whispered something, then handed her to Gavin.

Gavin placed her on Ella's chest. She cuddled the little one, never taking her eyes off. "Can someone bring Sarah up?"

"You might want to call the midwife too," Derek said. "See how close she is." His voice vibrated. "You need to deliver the placenta and I'm a little apprehensive to go that far."

I held his hand. "Let's go get Sarah and we can call the midwife. Let these two soak up this moment."

He followed me into the bathroom down the hall. I poured soap on his hands and rinsed them off, then turned off the water and looked at him. My eyes said two things. *I'm proud of you* and *I love you*. He must've read my mind because he pulled me into him and held me there. When he stepped back he kissed me and said, "That was one of the best moments of my life and I'm so thankful you were by my side."

"It was quite beautiful."

"It was." He nodded and smiled. "It really was."

Chapter Twenty Four
Derek

The next few weeks were a blur. The rush of new love and excitement. After the initial whirlwind, Miranda and I settled into a relationship. A normal, functional relationship. Our constant bickering from the early days ceased. We read books on science and life and discussed them for hours afterward, enjoying every second of each other. Every conversation between us sparked an interesting idea and a brand new conversation. We seemed to talk forever, like we needed to catch up after all the years without each other. And I loved every second of it. Never had I met a woman as intellectually engaging as Miranda. She challenged my thoughts and opinions because she never thought inside the box. I loved it. I loved her.

I moved into the city, three blocks away from her. After we unpacked my apartment she flopped onto the bed, her pink-streaked hair falling with her. I smiled inside and sat by her feet, scanning the room and grazing her body with my eyes.

"Well," she said. "What are you going to do with all the money?"

"I don't know. You keep asking about that."

"I think we should do something with it. Don't know what."

"I like keeping the envelopes in the car. I'd rather help a lot of people in small ways then do something big. I don't want any spotlight if that's what you're thinking."

"You should speak up about this, Derek. Write a book. I can help."

"No way."

"After all you've been through, do you honestly still believe abortion is okay?"

"Let's not talk about that."

"I'm serious. I want to know if you would still endorse it. What about a raped child? Fourteen years old and pregnant. Do you believe in abortion for her?"

I shook my head and exhaled. "You and your loaded questions."

"What is the story of your life if you never change?"

"This coming from the girl with pink hair."

"Have you changed?"

"I can't speak for the entire world. All I know is that for me . . . I don't ever want to be a part of an abortion again and I'm sorry I ever was. Yes, I feel like I've killed innocent lives, but I can't make the choice for everyone around me. Like you said, God doesn't force anyone to do good or bad. We have to make the choices that define our lives. The really difficult thing is that even if I see something as good, someone else may think it's horrible. I might see something as bad, but they're seeing it as good. We can't change people with our sap stories. Besides, it doesn't matter what my opinion is. Whether I agree with it or not, people need to make their own choices. I don't want to tell my emotional story in hopes of swaying people in one direction. If they can't come to it within themselves they'll just laugh at my story anyway." I took her hand. "I just want to be with you, move on from that life, and live a simple life together until we're old."

"Are you saying you want to marry me?"

"That goes without saying."

She smiled, kissed my hand, and wrapped her arms around me. We fell back into the pillows, laughing. She dug her sharp fingernails into my ribs, attempting to tickle me. I laughed and pushed her away. She grabbed a pillow and shoved it into my face. I grabbed another one and shoved it into my own face, pretending to throw myself off the bed. I landed on the floor and she peered down in hysterics. Our laughter filled the room as she jumped on top of me and dug her fingers into me again. I pushed her away and ticked her back until she begged for mercy. When I won and she gave up, we stayed on the floor, looking up at the ceiling like two snow angels holding hands.

After a few minutes of silence, she stood. "Be right back."

A few seconds later she returned to the room and set a gift on the floor beside me. I sat up and took it. "What's this for?"

"Just because."

I shook the box.

"Just open it," she said.

I unwrapped the brown paper to reveal a plain brown box underneath with the words Life is more colorful when you're in love. I laughed. "Nice one."

She smiled. "Open the box."

I opened it and pulled out a laminated flower. "Is this—?"

"I picked three flowers that day. I laminated each one, just in case I wanted to remember that kiss."

"Some kiss. Knocked you right off your feet."

She laughed. "I'll never forget that day. Those flowers. I know we aren't talking about the future and all, but I'd like to have my honeymoon there." She tapped my chest. "Not sure who I'm going to marry, but if I do get married, I'd like to have my honeymoon there and make love in that field of flowers."

Heat rushed through my body, causing sweat to instantly gather on my forehead. "Don't tempt me, little lady." I set the flower on my lap and took her hands. Her eyes brightened. I'd never seen her so happy, and for a moment, I caught my own reflection in her glassy eyes. I'd never seen myself so happy either. So content. "You've turned my life upside down. In a good way."

"I love you, Derek. I love you so much more than I ever thought I could love another person." Her eyes looked back and forth between my eyes. "Don't you ever make me regret this."

"I may not be William Wallace, but I plan to give this everything I've got."

She licked her lips and leaned toward mine. The chemistry between us spazzed out. I don't think chemistry could handle the sparks when our lips met. I don't think any word in the world could explain the way I felt with her. The closet thing I can think of, which in no way does it justice....

Electrifyingly content.

A knock boomed through the apartment. Miranda jumped. I stood and walked to the front door with her lagging behind me, her fingertips in the palm of my hand. Who could be at my door? I just moved here. Miranda seemed perplexed too, and when I opened the door we both dropped our jaws to the floor.

Her father stepped into my apartment, took off his Pittsburgh Pirates hat, and said, "May I?"

I ushered him toward the couches which were covered in boxes. I shoved a few aside and made room for the three of us. We all sat down, then he stood back up. "I can't stay long." He rolled his hat between his hands, then looked at us with a pained expression. "Look, I came here to apologize. To both of you." He looked at me, still switching the hat from hand to hand. "I thought about what you said and you're right." He looked at Miranda and put his hat back on. A shadow hovered over his eyes. "Miranda, you are my daughter and I'm sorry. I wasn't the father you needed. I wasn't the husband your mother needed. I wasn't much of anything for anyone and it took a while to realize it." He stepped toward the door and turned back to us. "I'm trying to get help."

He extended his hand to me and shook, then reached for Miranda's hand, but she wrapped her arms around his shoulders and pressed her cheek against his chest. He jerked and bit his lip. I looked at my feet.

"Not every story has a perfect ending," he said. "But I want to do my best to make my story turn out a little better. You know, I started thinking . . . at my funeral what would my memory be? When my dad died I was twelve years old, raised to be tough and suck it up, but during his funeral they couldn't find me. I was hiding under his casket shaking so hard I almost knocked the thing over. When he died I lost something and I'm afraid if I died right now people wouldn't lose anything, they'd gain something. That's not what I want." He shook his head and stepped back into the room, away from the door. "When my father died I remembered fun times. I remembered playing ball and breaking in my gloves. I'm sorry I haven't given you good memories, Miranda. I want to make it better. I want to die a better man than the one I've been. I've been through a lot." He squeezed his eyes shut as though in pain. "But it's no excuse . . . it's no excuse. . . ."

"Dad," she said, peering up at him through strands of tear-soaked hair. "I always loved you. We all did. That's why you hurt us so much, because we loved you so much." More tears. "I'm sorry too. I'm sorry for all of the horrible things I've said throughout my life. I wasn't the best kid in the world and I know that."

"You're my daughter. I know I've never said this before since you've come into the world, but I want you to hear it now. And it's not easy for me to say it. For some reason it feels like pulling hair, but I need to say it." He drew in a breath. "I love you." And with that he nodded his head, tipped his hat to me, and put one hand on the door knob. "Thank you both."

He closed the door behind him. Miranda and I moved to the front window, peeled back the curtains, and watched him saunter away with his head up.

She leaned into my arms and sniffed. "I can't believe it."

"I can't either," I said. "I think I'm still in shock."

"You know, sometimes I wonder if more people would change if we only believed in them." She let go of the curtains and faced me. "We are so trained into believing the worst, into thinking some people are beyond hope. What if it's our lack of belief that makes people hopeless? What if we can change the world just by hoping for the best instead of settling for the worst?"

I kissed her forehead and pulled her into me. "I've never known anyone like you, Liz."

"I'm serious though."

"I know you are. And I love you for it."

Chapter Twenty Five
Miranda

nother lonely park bench called my name. It's wrought iron frame, wooden slats, and desire to hold another life filled with wonder. I sat down and admired the passing strangers. One by one they entered my life, if only for a brief moment, then exited. Kids licking ice cream off their chins. Teens running their thumbs down their phone screens. Business people briskly walking to their appointments. Couples stopping to kiss underneath the arms of a tree. Life. Passing by. Inspiring me, once again, to pull out my journal. I reclined on the bench, pressed my blue-tipped pen into the paper, and began at the place most stories leave off.

And they lived happily ever after....

Most love stories begin with "once upon a time" and end with "happily ever after." Not Turtle and Lizzy. Their "once upon time" happened to be the beginning of their friendship, but not the beginning of their love story.

Both Turtle and Lizzy suffered from the same illness disguised in different ways. Lizzy spent her life feeling unworthy of love, so she shut down and turned herself into a revolving door and tried to blend in to her latest attraction. Turtle, on the other hand, made a few wrong decisions and became someone he couldn't stand, so he reverted to his shell and deemed himself unworthy of the love he so desired.

Fear.

That was their illness. They feared themselves. Feared others. Feared opinions, rejections, and, well, each other.

But they didn't give up. They tried to, but didn't know how. So Turtle helped Lizzy learn how to find her own colors instead of being such a chameleon all the time. Lizzy also helped Turtle. He would say she helped him become a man, a real Turtle man. But Lizzy doesn't see it that way. She believes she simply helped him discover the boy in him. Because to her, it's the boy in the man that makes a man so valiant.

Either way, the love between them broke down the walls around their hearts and for the first time in their lives they opened up to another person. Let someone in. Loved. Really loved.

So, how can we start the Turtle and Lizzy story with "happily ever after?" Easy. Because when two people finally find the courage to do something they've been fearing for so long ... they will fight forever to keep the gift they've been given. Because now, it's no longer opening up that they fear... It's losing the one they've let in.

HE SAT DOWN BY MY FEET AND SMILED AT ME. SERENE, SOOTH-ing. A few months ago the very presence of one another made us both uneasy. Now we felt at home. My best friend turned into my boyfriend and I knew without a doubt, when the time was right, we'd naturally find ourselves as husband and wife.

I locked my fingers with his and smiled. "I'll never let you go. You know that, right? You're stuck with me forever now."

He draped his arm over my knee and grabbed my other hand. "Can't think of someone better to be stuck to."

"You know." I sat up and snuggled into his chest. "I sat on this bench so many times. Wondering if I'd get married. If I'd let someone in and if that person would actually like what they found." I leaned up and kissed his cheek. "Now, I'm sitting here with you and looking at the girl on that bench over there."

"Where?"

I pointed. "She reminds me of myself. I've been watching her since I got here. She's been watching others. Like I do. I can't help but wonder if she's looking at us and fashioning her own ideals as she imagines our love story unfolding before her eyes."

"Well." He laughed. "Not everyone has an imagination like you. You wonder far more than the average person."

"Yes." I ripped a blank paper out of my journal. "I have an idea."

"That reminds me. Now that I'm living here I need you to help me figure out what I should do for my job."

"Live off your savings?"

He laughed. "You know I don't feel right spending all that on myself. Plus I need a job. Something to do."

"Maybe deliver babies?"

He gazed into the distance. Probably imagining his son.

"Think happy thoughts. Replace all of your bad memories with good ones. Bring life into the world."

"What was your idea with the paper?"

"Let's leave notes on benches. Every time I sit on a bench I want to leave something behind."

"Meaning?"

I drew a heart then tore around the edges. Still had an extra red shoe string in my purse, so I looped it through a hole in the heart and handed it to Derek. "Write something on it."

"Like what?"

"Anything. Something that will inspire the person who sits here next."

He took my pen and thought about it.

"Don't think too hard," I said. "Might hurt yourself."

"I have no idea what to write."

"Come on. Be inspiring." I tapped his head. "Feel the inspiration. Be the inspiration."

"Very funny." He took the cap off the pen. "Still clueless."

"Imagine a young guy sitting down here after a long day at school. He's a senior in high school. Scholarship to every university imaginable, but he feels empty. Lonely. Now, tell him something. A quick word of inspiration

155

that will spark his heart and bring him to life."

"You're something else. You know that?"

I pointed to the heart. His pen touched the paper, grazed it with gentle strokes, and formed a small paragraph. He put the cap back on the pen and handed me the heart.

If anyone is going to be the villain in your story, don't let it be yourself. When you find the right one, give her all of you, not just the good parts, the scraps too. Let her into the worst and if she still loves you, keep her. Jump off the bridge. Leap across the canyon. Fly. You won't die, and if you do, it's a good kind of death anyway. Life is waiting on the other side.

I smiled. "Perfect." We stood. I hung the shoe string on the back of the bench so the heart dangled in front. We stepped back, admired our work, and then admired each other.

He took my hand and led me away from the bench. The cool breeze flipped the leaves on the trees, making way for another summer storm, possibly the last before autumn covered the stage of life with a new backdrop. Birds chirped above us, people jogged with headphones in their ears, and the girl with a sweet sparkle in her eyes grinned as we passed her. Strangers crossing paths. Our eyes met and I could see hope beneath her gaze. Like damp soil warmed after a germinating winter, ready and eager for life. Ready for anything. Something.

Derek swayed our hands as our feet stepped to the same rhythm, carrying us into a dream where princes donned themselves in brown t-shirts and princesses had pink hair and laceless shoes. Together, we inhaled the present and exhaled the future. Every moment meant something. Every action counted. Another memory in our story. Another page in our book. The story we'd write side-by-side until the moon no longer glowed on our faces, but lit our names on neighboring gravetones.

Somehow, someway, I became a story passing by another. A story worth reading. I never thought I'd be so happy to walk away from my beloved park bench.

Love not only changes lives ... it gives birth to life.

And I made it my life goal to never go a day without treasuring life with him by my side.

The best and most beautiful things in the world cannot be seen or even touched. They must be felt with the heart.
Helen Keller

A beautiful, successful, sweet personality with the world at her fingertips, **Sarah Jordan** falls in love with James, a charming man who adores her. But he comes with broken pieces and a daughter he adopted when his brother and sister-in-law died in an accident he feels he could've prevented. When she finally decides to say "yes" to his many proposals, they are both burned in a campfire accident. After a year of hospital beds and stark lights, Sarah is released to go home with everything but her former beauty. As she recovers, James struggles with regret and guilt as Sarah fights to overcome the depression that comes with a new life so different from the one she loved so much. Her joy and security are tested while budding relationships cleanse wounds they never knew they had.

Coming May 2014

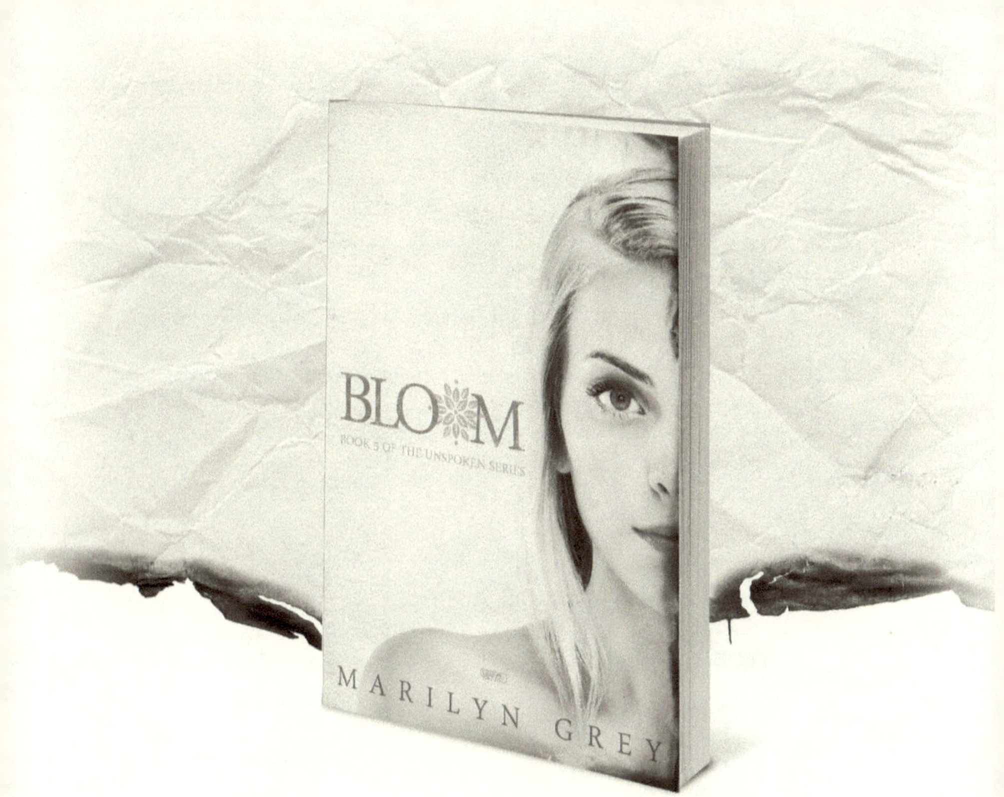

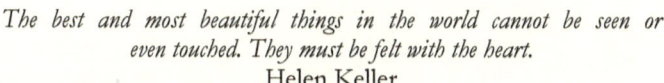

Bloom

Sarah's Story

Prologue
August
a year and a half prior

JAMES AND I MADE S'MORES BY THE FIRE. ALWAYS A CAREFUL person, I stayed three feet away from the crackling flames as I roasted my marshmallow, then smothered it between chocolate and crunchy graham crackers. James wiped my face and kissed the side of my mouth. We spent an hour talking about life. Our goals. Our future.

Near the end of the conversation I yawned. He got down on his knees to clean up the boxes and trash. At least that's what I thought.

Staring up at me, he took something out of his pocket. I straightened my back as I sat on the log and a smile wrapped around my face as he took my hand.

"Sarah, we've both been through a lot. I know I'm not like all of your friends. I'm normal. A mechanic. Not artsy like you and all of them. I've argued with myself constantly. Had this ring for a while, you know." He spun it in his hands, looking down. "I didn't know how to make this romantic and over the top. I didn't want to ask for help either because, to me, that's a lie. This is who I am. I may not be the most romantic guy in the world, but you're my best friend and I want to experience life with you. Forever. So ... what do you think?"

I covered my mouth as he slipped the ring on my left hand. "Of course, James. You know my concerns about leaving Abby though. She can't lose a mother figure twice. It would be unbearable."

"Your cancer is gone. Doctors say there's a good chance it's gone forever."

I nodded. "Enough of that talk. I want to relish this moment. I never want to forget the way it felt when you asked me to be your wife."

He stood and pulled me into his arms. "How does it feel?"

"It feels ... normal."

We laughed. He carried me into the tent and flopped me onto the pillows. We had a ton of cheap three-dollar pillows stuffed in the tent. James surprised me because I once told him I wanted to sleep on a cloud.

"Can you go put out the fire?" I said.

He smiled. "Yes. Right after I kiss my future wife."

We kissed as the moonlight lit our faces. That's the last wonderful thing I remember before waking up to James screaming for me.

By the time I opened my eyes the tent was orange and a horrible scent clung to my nose. I screamed and backed into the corner of the tent, looking for James as the bed of clouds engulfed into huge flames. I closed my eyes and covered my face with my arm as I clawed at the tent, trying to rip the cloth and bite my way out of the fabric. The flames licked my skin, inching closer.

I looked down at my legs and hands. Didn't take long to realize. The ghastly smell was my own skin melting off. Sharp bursts of pain seared through every inch of my body. Skin, black like the marshmallow I burned a little while ago, flapped off my arm and I could see the bone in my left hand, where the ring he gave me no longer resided.

James screamed my name again. A haunting chill swept over me, cooling my inflamed body. I collapsed in the corner of the tent like a parachute falling to the ground and asked God to take me quickly. A rush of sunny memories terrified me. I'd never see them again. This was the end.

Then each memory vanished and the world turned black.

Chapter One

MY ROOM SMELLED OF BUTTERY PANCAKES AND PUMPKIN PIE. I turned on my phone. 9:32a.m. September 15th. I no longer needed help taking off my burn mask. Thankfully. No need to wake Cheyenne this morning, who was still sleeping peacefully in the twin bed beside mine. Ella had been an angel. Not only allowing me to stay in her home, but allowing my cousin Cheyenne to stay with me as well. Ella worried that she wouldn't be able to help me after she had the baby, but Adelaide Kessler was four weeks and two days old and Ella spent four weeks and one day out of those first weeks of her daughters life checking on me every three hours. At least.

I stayed in the hospital longer than most of the other burn unit patients. Partly because I had a lot of infections along the way, near death experiences, and trouble learning to walk again. And also because I wanted to. I feared coming home and burdening others. I feared being needy and, most of all, I feared that I'd no longer be able to hide my tears. When someone visited me in the hospital I had enough warning to dry my eyes and put on a happy face. In the world I'd need to hold it in or let it out. And let it known.

Cheyenne stirred and saw me standing without my burn mask. "You're getting quite ambitious, aren't you?"

"Funny," I said. "Gone are the days when ten mile runs were ambitious. Now getting out of bed myself is an accomplishment."

"You've come so far since the accident. Imagine how normal life will be by this time next year."

I toddled toward the bathroom. Ignoring her optimism. I knew the heart of an optimist well. I used to be one. My entire life. Until now. But normal wouldn't exist for me ever again. A new normal, maybe. But not my old normal.

Cheyenne closed the bathroom door behind me. "Let me know if you need help."

I stood in front of the mirror. Someone's face stared back at me. Red, swollen, and disfigured. The right side of my face remained somewhat normal, but the left side ... I looked away and positioned myself on the toilet. Took ten minutes to do something I once did in two. I washed my hands and avoided the mirror.

Throughout my life people complimented my beauty, but honestly, I never though much of it. I didn't get too into my looks like some girls. Wasn't important to me.

Every time I saw my reflection in a mirror I couldn't help but realize how important it actually was to me. I just didn't realize it until it was gone.

Life with a different face is a new life altogether. People treated me like a child now. They talked to me with loud and slow voices as though my ears melted away in the fire. Strangers stared and kids pointed. Men, who once turned their heads to watch me walk away, now turned their heads in disgust. I never needed attention. And I still didn't. Maybe that's why it upset me to be looked at so much.

Cheyenne knocked on the door. "Everything okay? Ready to change your dressings?"

I opened the door.

"And here are your pills."

She placed them in my palm on top of the cloth surrounding my hand. I put them in my mouth one at a time and gulped the water she gave me.

"Well," she said. "Ella made baked pumpkin oatmeal for breakfast. Would you like some?"

"No, thanks."

"You need to eat more, Sarah."

Cheyenne was not only my cousin. She was a nurse. And sometimes I wished she weren't.

"Let's change this stuff," I said. "Get my ever dreaded shower and get through the morning routine. Maybe after that I will eat lunch."

Cheyenne entered the bathroom and closed the door. Ella and Gavin chatted downstairs. I could hear them discussing work and lessons as silverware clanged in the sink. I imagined Adelaide snuggled against her chest in the baby wrap and Gavin's arms around them both, wondering if I'd ever be able to have children. If so, I wouldn't be able to nurse them. My flat chest with weird skin caught my eye as Cheyenne helped me undress. Mirrors insulted me, especially when unclothed. So I stepped aside and closed my eyes.

The pain, still intense, seemed as though it would remain with me for the rest of my life. "Poor James."

"Not poor James. He loves you."

"Did I say that aloud?"

She nodded as she completed her task and I took slow steps into the shower. I so dreaded the shower.

"Looks aren't everything, Sarah. They aren't even close."

Easy for her to say. She still had her beauty. I didn't even have breasts to nurse a child with. The doctor mentioned plastic surgery, but the thought appalled me.

"I'm like a child," I said. "He needs a wife. Not a child."

She turned on the water and I flinched.

"He needs you," she said. "Period."

Cheyenne helped me finish my painful morning routine in silence, then she asked me if I'd be okay with her leaving for a while. I nodded from my bed. Sleep called for me. Especially after those torturous showers.

MY DREAMS EITHER INVOLVED BEING TRAPPED IN A BURNING building or a mangled car. So I didn't sleep much, but this time I dreamt of James and Abby with a woman who could take care of them. When I awoke James was sitting beside me smiling. "Morning, beautiful."

"How can you say beautiful?" I said, closing my eyes again.

He didn't respond. I looked at him again. His smile disappeared. Replaced by two serious eyes and turned down lips.

"Abby deserves better, James. So do you."

He unhooked the necklace around his neck and placed it on the table by my bed. The ring clanked as it hit the wood. James touched my shoulder. "I'm sticking by you until that ring goes back on your finger with a wedding band."

"James."

"Sarah."

"You don't have to feel sorry for me. Don't do this out of pity or guilt. I'm a big girl."

He stood. "Every time I visit. Every single time you try to get rid of me. I'm doing the best I can. What do you want from me?"

"You don't want to marry me. Admit it. If you met me now you'd never think twice about putting a ring on my finger." I held back tears. "You're worried about Abby. I get that. Since your brother died and Abby lost her parents, you feel like you need to protect her. That's true. You're her daddy now and she needs you. But she also needs a mother. A real one. Let me go,

James. Just let me go. I don't want pity."

His eyes narrowed. "I've been by your bed every moment possible since this happened. Is this your way of saying thanks?"

"I am thankful." I looked down. "You're a wonderful person. You've been good to me. But I'm okay. It wasn't your fault and you can walk away without hurting me. I'll be okay."

"What would you have said if we were already married and this happened, huh? What then?"

I stared at my bare chest. The chest that was meant to nurse my children during sleepless nights. Gone. My dreams of motherhood melted away in that fire. I'd failed my children before giving birth to them.

I loved James too much to see him settle for me just because he loved the person I was before all of this. Maybe one day he would understand it was my love for him that helped me let him go.

He stood in the doorway. "You know that scene from Titantic?"

I shook my head.

"Come on, you've made me watch it six times."

"Which scene?"

"The one."

"Please don't, James."

"I've been by your side since this happened. You almost died twice and that kind of thing makes you realize a lot. Made me realize that I may be able to go on living without you, but I don't want to." He closed the door. His footsteps trailed off. I heard the car door close and the engine rumble.

The door opened again.

Ella sat a few scones and a steaming cup of tea on the table beside me.

"I know what you're going to say," I said. "Don't say it."

She smiled. "What am I going to say?"

"That I need to be nice to him, but you don't understand. I need him to let go. For his own good. If I'm nice he'll hang on."

"I don't know what's going on between you two. You never say anything and he's as private as you are." She handed me a blueberry-orange scone. "I was going to reprimand you for not eating. You have to if you want to get better."

I picked off a piece and chewed it. Pretty good actually. "Change of pace, huh?"

"What do you mean?"

"Me, depressed. You, cheery." I laughed. "Tables have turned."

"You remember what you said to me once?" She tapped my foot. "My dream is every day. When I wake up, I want to find something new. Something beautiful about each day I'm given. I want to take the cards I'm given and play them with a smile, not to win, just to play."

"Yeah. I said that when life's biggest disappointment was losing a job or being single."

"Well, try it." She stood, left, and returned with the baby. "Find something beautiful."

"It's hard, Ella. I see negative in everything. There you are holding a baby and instead of seeing her beauty and your happiness all I see is my inability to have children and it makes me not want to be around either of you."

"Doctor never said you can't have children."

"What kind of man wants to marry a woman with a shriveled up chest?"

"The man you have." She glanced at the glistening ring on my night stand. "He wants you."

I closed my eyes and remembered the first time I opened them after the accident. I didn't know where I was and when I did I wished I had died. For months after that, wrapped up like a mummy, I kept wishing I'd close my eyes and die of an infection. People came in and out of my room. Checked my catheter. Did my excruciating physical therapy. Had conversations about their boyfriends and girlfriends and lives outside of the hospital. The life I wanted to crawl back to.

I should've never went camping. Should've made him put the fire out. Shouldn't have fallen asleep. Endless regrets always ran through my head.

I tried to remain positive. That's what people expected of me. Always the sunshine in the room. I didn't want to let people down. Or maybe I didn't want to let myself down. Why is being fake easier than being real?

I opened my eyes. Ella smiled, sat in the chair across the room, and nursed Adelaide.

Knife in my non-existent chest.

I winced. "When you're finished could you give me some pain medication?"

She nodded.

"And do you mind not nursing her in front of me?"

A tear slipped down her face. "Sarah, I love you, but I'm not going to hide life from you. Yes, I can nurse a baby and you may never be able to, but there are many things you can do that I will never do. Think about who you are and how this can be turned into something good. So, you can't nurse a child. Adopt one. Do something. Think of others. Count your blessings."

My phone made a sound. I picked it up with the hand that didn't get burned. The hand I could still type and write with. A notification. Physical therapy in two hours. Great.

Ella already knew. She nodded when I looked at her and said, "Let's get you ready to go."

"Where's Gavin?"

"In the studio. Today's homeschooler day. He's teaching a few art classes and I have a few private violin lessons later. It's fine. I can take Adelaide."

"I can get Cheyenne."

"Sarah Jordan, I'm taking you. Soon you won't need help anymore and you'll be so busy that you won't have time to read. Enjoy this while it lasts."

I inched myself into a sitting position and sat on the edge of the bed. "Maybe I'd enjoy it a little more if I wasn't in constant pain."

"You've made it this far."

"This is so hard, Ella. It's so hard. I felt okay until I came home. Or to your home. Now life is going on all around me and every time I look in the mirror I want to cry."

She placed Adelaide in a baby wrap and put her arm around me. "I've always admired you, Sarah. And I still do. Throughout all of this you still manage to laugh and smile. You don't tell everyone how hard it is and you put on this positive mask, but underneath you really are that person. These moments of sadness are normal. What I admire is that you still smile more than you cry."

"Thank you for that." I smiled. "Let's go."

Your Questions Answered

Q. What made you decide to write romance novels over other genres?

A. I think because I'm a huge romantic at heart and it comes so natural for me. I do have a love for conspiracy books and I think I might do that at some point. Also a dystopian idea, but that wouldn't fit into a series. The Unspoken Series was inspired by Downton Abbey. I wanted to write something that I would like to read. Something beautiful and not sex, sex, sex. So, I created this series to be my ideal little romantic world and I was inspired by Downton Abbey's brilliant way of incorporating so many lives and stories into one big story. So, here I am! I love doing it and this series is an absolute joy to write.

Q. If you had to pick someone to play Ella and Gavin for a movie, who would you pick?

A. What a fun question! That's tough. My favorite actors are too old for those roles or wouldn't work. I love Benedict Cumberbatch, Dan Stevens, Kate Winslet, and Joaquin Phoenix. I think they are truly the best actors of our time. But they aren't Ella and Gavin. Ahhh, I really don't know!

Q. What books inspire your stories?

A. All kinds. It really depends on the book. As a whole, Charles Martin is incredibly gifted (in my opinion) and he has shaped my desire to write from the heart. I can't sing his praises enough. As for books that specifically inspire stories, it depends. For Mwenye's story I've watched a lot of movies about slavery. *Amistad* is a favorite. *The Green Mile* is an inspiration in his story. Also, Maya Angelou and others who have spoken up for the beauty and strength of those with darker skin. *Heart on a Shoestring* was inspired by *Big Fish*, *Eternal Sunshine of the Spotless Mind*, and other oddities. I read a lot of non-fiction and believe it or not ... that inspires me the most. Real life is what provokes me to write. So that's what I like to read too.

Q. What inspires you to write? I love your emotional scenes, like the simple beauty of Gavin's wedding and their first night as husband and wife. How do you make them so realistic?

A. Life inspires me. I base a lot of these character's off of my own life or people I know, but of course they become their own person. I just analyze life around me, try to soak it in and let it come out in the written word. Gavin's wedding and scenes like that just come out naturally. I really have no idea how. I'm glad they seem realistic and people often say they feel like they know my characters. I consider them friends, so I'm glad others do as well! I just write from the heart so I guess the heart is what people get.

Q. This book was intense and somewhat controversial. Did something in your life inspire it?

A. Not really. I've known people who've had abortions, but nothing really inspired. These people jump out of the page and into my head ... I just help them get onto the page. I didn't really have an agenda with this or antyhing, just kind of happened and quite honestly, it gripped me and held me there. These two characters made me think!

Q. How can I get free books? I'm obsessed with this series!

A. Apply for my street team. Details are on my website!

Q. What's next?

A. Bloom is in its final stages and will be released in May. Publisher is still deciding whether to get Mwenye's story out after that or Nora's first. Guess we'll see!

Q. What's your favorite thing about books?

A. The smell. The feeling as you turn a page. I don't like to crease my books or bend corners. I don't idolize them or anything, but there's something about a smooth page. I could never trade my lovely paperback books for an electronic device. I love the feeling too much. Nothing like opening a new book and sniffing those pages. Am I the only weird one?

If you have any questions you'd like to see answered in the next book, please email them to Marilyn at marilyn@marilyn-grey.com and we'll select some to answer. You will also receive an answer from her via email. She adores her fans and responds to every email she receives.

Do you love The Unspoken Series?

Don't forget to connect with Marilyn on
Facebook, Twitter, and GoodReads. She is so excited
to hear from fans and talk about the characters
in *The Unspoken Series* with everyone!